HANDMADE MURDER

a novel

EMMA CHAPMAN

ISBN (paperback) 979-8-9893189-0-2
ISBN (hardback) 979-8-9893189-1-9
ISBN (ebook) 979-8-9893189-2-6

For my son, Oscar.

The idea for this book began to form in my mind when I was longing for you and in a dark place. I will never be able to put into words how much you changed my life. Thank you for making me a mother. I love you forever.

DEAR READER,

This book deals with many different themes but a big one is miscarriage. Considering how common it is, it's strange to me there isn't more art made about it. Longing and loss are painful feelings we might want to dismiss, or it can feel like our culture is dismissive of them. If you have suffered loss in this way, or in any way, please take care of yourself. You are important. You matter. For me, therapy has been immensely beneficial. Here are some things to consider if you or a loved one are going through the grief process:

Therapy or grief counseling – This could be someone you find online, in person or through a community that is important to you. Talking does help.

Consider memorializing the baby – Miscarriage feels like losing a child. Acknowledging pregnancy loss in a way that is meaningful to you is a healthy and appropriate way to grieve. This doesn't have to be a public event, but if you want to have a service you should.

Suicide and Crisis Lifeline – If you are having harmful thoughts, call or text 988 anytime of day or night (USA). This service is confidential and will connect you with a mental health professional. There is no shame in having thoughts like this. Get help if you need it. You are worth it.

CHAPTER 1

Joan sat down in the stool the guard directed her to. The metal chair squeaked as she pushed it back just enough for her to sit down. The noise felt loud and intrusive. Joan froze for a second, like a deer in headlights. The inmate Joan had come to see was already sitting across, the smudged plexiglass between them. Joan nodded to her and picked up the phone, hoping this gesture came off as a normal greeting. But there was nothing normal about these circumstances. Joan held the phone to her ear, realizing she hadn't used a landline phone in probably a decade and it felt strange and bulky. For nearly a whole minute the woman just stared back at her, no expression on her face. Joan wondered if she might get up and leave; maybe she had changed her mind? But then she picked up her phone too.

"Hello Joan. Nice to see you again," she said. Joan thought maybe she should say nice to see you too, but it felt wrong somehow, so she didn't.

"Hello. Thank you for agreeing to speak with me," Joan said.

"You're the only journalist I've agreed to talk to. I'm sure you know this already."

"Honestly, I didn't," Joan paused, she was a little unsure what to say to this. "How are you doing, in here?" She immediately wished she'd left off the 'in here' part.

"In prison? Oh, well, better than you might think I guess. They treat me pretty well, but I suspect this will change some months from now considering my condition."

"Right. Well, still, that's good for now anyway." What was she saying? But as soon as she had walked in she'd felt so sorry for this woman, despite everything. The whole thing was a huge waste and too sad to look at head-on. And Joan felt it was somewhat her fault.

"I assume you have questions for me? Not to be rude, but I'd rather just get on with it if that's OK," the woman said, not unkindly. She looked tired and a little pale. Joan noticed her hair had grown out some and she now had ashy blonde roots peeking out of her brunette locks.

"Sure. Let's get into it," she shuffled some notes, she felt unsure where to start now. She knew she wasn't in charge of the interview and she needed to be, perhaps she'd skip the obviously warm-up type questions and just dive in deeper. "Were the packages meant to be gifts?"

"Which ones?" the woman asked without hesitation.

"All of them I guess. But you usually sent two, right?" Joan asked.

"They were all gifts. The first was more obvious, a comfort or a keepsake. The second was a key."

"What do you mean a key?" Joan asked, puzzled.

"It was a way out. A key. A door. An alternate ending. A second chance."

"I don't think any of your victims saw it that way,"

"Well, we haven't heard from all of them, so I guess neither of us really knows. But that's what I intended, which I think should count for something," the woman said.

"Do you still view it that way? You were setting them free?"

The woman didn't answer for a long time, she looked like she was in a trance. Joan wondered if she might start crying. But then her face came to life again.

"I think my views on it have shifted some. But mostly I am proud to have inspired more interesting conversations. I'm also kind of shocked how obsessed people seem to be with me, or the idea of me. The media seems more excited about me than OJ and Dahmer combined. I must be paying a lot of their bills."

"Do you like being famous?" Joan asked. Keeping her tone neutral, curious.

"I like feeling important. I think most people do. And I'm sure you can understand. I mean, how many downloads did your podcast get when you released my story? Did it make you feel like you were doing something important?" the woman asked. She seemed to actually expect an answer.

"Yeah. I guess it did," Joan admitted. Why lie? Then, "Do you know how many times you were successful? Did you keep some kind of record?"

"I kept track of things, but there were always factors I couldn't control. Much like life. So, I did what I did but I didn't worry myself too much about the results. That part wasn't up to me, that part was up to the universe."

"So, then, have you been surprised by what the prosecution has shown in court so far?"

"Hmm. Yeah, I guess I would say it has surprised me. I was even more successful than I had hoped. I take it as a sign."

"What do you mean?" Joan asked.

"Just, it must be a sign that I was on the right track. I was doing the work I was meant to do."

"You felt called, like by God or another entity, to do this?"

"I feel pretty agnostic about God, but maybe. Do you think we're all meant to do something? Like when you see a performer at a concert and it just clicks why everyone is obsessed with their music. You

5

can see it when you look at them. They are doing what they are meant to do in this world. Look at me," the woman paused. She waited until Joan looked up into her eyes; she had been taking notes. "What do you think? Am I doing what I was meant to do?"

Joan didn't answer. But she knew what the woman meant, what it was like seeing someone be the thing they were meant for. And she'd seen it when people didn't have it, that weird extra ingredient that was hard to articulate but easy to see. And Joan felt a little jolt of electricity run up her spine because she knew this woman had it.

"Why did you agree to talk to me?" Joan asked, putting her pen down.

"I liked your podcast. I thought it was honest. I don't really care about getting 'my side of the story' out or whatever. But I do resent being made into a character, like I'm here just to fill time and airwaves and pad rich media conglomerates' pockets. Media is kind of a joke if you ask me. No offense. But your podcast, it was good. It was honest. You might be a little bit of a liar, but your story was the truth."

Although Joan could tell she'd meant this as a compliment, it didn't really feel like one. Joan didn't feel the story was complete. She felt she hadn't told the whole story yet and she desperately wanted to.

"Do you ever feel misunderstood?" Joan asked. She had actually been feeling this herself in the moment, thinking about the reaction to her podcast. But then she wondered if this woman didn't feel the same way, but for different reasons.

"Yes. Very much actually. See, I knew you got it. That's all I think when I see those women in court. The 'sea of victims' as the media has started calling them. Very dehumanizing really. I actually know all of their names, or at least what they call themselves online."

"Really? You see them in court and you know each of their names? There are a lot of them."

"Yes, I do. And I know about their lives, or at least what they put out there on the internet. It's not hard to know them, they make a living of being known. And yet the media keeps coming up with terms to turn them into this big glob or something. And I'm the fucking villain."

Joan actually agreed. Murderers have always sold more papers, or gotten more clicks, than victims. And yet, here she was talking to this woman rather than the victims. She was no better, she thought. Joan wanted to get the interview back on track and get out of here. The room felt both hot and cold, and she could feel a sickly kind of sweat starting to form on her lower back. She wanted to leave as soon as possible.

"Well, if you feel misunderstood I'd like to hear why. I know you said you don't care about getting out your side of the story, but maybe you can tell me more, from your point of view, why you did it," Joan said.

She could see the wheels turning in the woman's head, thinking or maybe calculating how long it would take and if it was worth the effort. Joan almost hoped she wouldn't, which was very un-journalist of her. The whole story had gotten under her skin in a way she knew she wouldn't get over for a long time, maybe ever.

"You know what Joan, I think I'll pass for now. I like you, well, I also dislike you for obvious reasons. But you had a job to do and I think you did it with conviction. I did too. And although it's very tempting to try and explain myself, and show how what I've done was right, it also feels kind of. Hmm, how to put this? It feels like a deranged man trying to write a manifesto. I don't actually think I'm all that important. I did what I did. The world can decide what they think of it now, and ultimately what to do with a woman like me."

Then the woman got up and left. Leaving Joan still holding her side of the phone to her ear. She had never been in charge of this interview, but it felt almost poetically fair considering the last time they had met. Joan watched her as she left the room and was cuffed again. The woman smiled and tipped her chin up, like an old friend saying goodbye.

Joan was lost in her thoughts as she collected her things and was directed back toward the parking lot. She had thought she'd be relieved when the interview was over, but she wasn't. She'd only visited a prison a few times for a story, and it was always a lot of anticipation as there were many steps: getting on the list, getting checked by the authorities, ultimately being approved to visit and then securing a date. She always felt nervous something would go wrong, or she'd be denied, so when she finally got through the process it was a relief—like making it to your destination after a very long series of flights with tight connections. But now she had more questions than when she had gone in. She didn't feel relief, she felt off balance.

She had parked her rental car toward the back of the lot, and as she reached it, she heard someone call her name. And then more shouts of her name. She turned to look toward the gate that led out of the prison lot, and she could see a dozen or more news vans parked with journalists filming with the prison behind them. And many of them turning to try to get her attention as Joan left. How did they even know she was here? It looked more like a movie premiere than the outside of a federal prison. She remembered what the woman had said, that she must be paying a lot of people's bills for how obsessed they were with her story. Joan felt sick and a little betrayed. These were her peers, but it felt like a circus and she was the performer. Nothing about this was what she had wanted from her career. She felt an overwhelming sense of despair, and she felt like quitting. What a high note to quit on too. But something itched in the back of her mind, she knew the story wasn't done with her yet. And she knew where to look next.

CHAPTER 2

Ela
@justanotherela

| **58** POSTS | **599** FOLLOWERS | **592** FOLLOWING |

She had never enjoyed being naked, and now was no exception. Ela watched as the water turned a deep foamy turquoise, the bath bomb releasing its potent mix of smells and colors. The water fizzed back at her in response to a question she hadn't asked, as she carefully lowered herself into the tub. She was careful not to catch a glimpse of her naked torso in the mirror, which was quite an accomplishment given the size of their 1920s bungalow bathroom. She was beginning her second trimester, but she hadn't yet noticed any changes to her stomach. The doctor had assured her at the last appointment this was still normal and that it would happen soon, but nothing so far.

Her phone buzzed at the edge of the tub. She probably shouldn't bring her phone into the bathroom, but she sometimes liked to scroll Instagram while she soaked. Her husband's name flashed across the screen. Luckily, he wasn't trying to FaceTime her, since she didn't feel in the mood for a naked FaceTime chat.

"Hi," she answered.

"Hey Ela. Just calling to check in on you. I'm about to go into a meeting but I wanted to see how you were feeling?" James asked. She noted he didn't want to talk long, so he chose to call at a strategic time. He could hop off quickly for his conference meeting. Cool.

"I'm fine. Just having a bath." She answered flatly. Hearing her tone, she realized she might be acting a touch uncharitable. She decided to change course.

"How's the conference? Anything of note so far? Is your hotel interesting?" She rattled off a few questions, letting him decide what to answer.

"Not really. There was a mix up, so Phil and I are sharing a twin room, which is fine by me. I think Phil was more disappointed," he answered with a good-natured chuckle.

"What's the next talk you're hearing?" Ela asked.

"It's about working with *influencers*," he said with a little laugh. "I'm all for any marketing strategy that sees a decent ROI for the client, but I wish they were called something other than influencers."

"What would be better? Bloggers? Vloggers? Instagram girls?" she asked with a smile. She agreed it was a sort of silly name, but the whole thing was hard to take seriously and yet there it was. She followed lots of influencers and had often bought things they talked about, she had to admit.

"You're right. It's not their fault they got unlucky in the title department. Well, it looks like everyone is taking their seats, so I better jump off," James said.

"OK. Thanks for calling. Love you."

"Love you too."

She set her phone on the far edge of the tub, away from the water's edge. She'd slightly overfilled it, and she was afraid if she moved around too much the water might slosh out. She leaned her head back, replaying the conversation. She had been pleasant enough, she thought. Really, she wanted James home more. If he wasn't out of town for work, he was at the office late or having a very late-into-the-night happy hour with coworkers. It was hard to imagine him being home more in just six months, helping her with a newborn. She loved James, but the thought of him being a family man was difficult to picture. She just hoped everything would fall into place. It had taken a few years to conceive and along the way he had gone back and forth, getting cold feet at moments, which gutted her each time. Friends and family had told her not to worry, sometimes men don't feel like fathers until they hold their child in their arms. But this struck her as rather late to the game, didn't it? At that point, it would be impossible to change your mind without looking like a complete asshole. Still. She hoped they were right.

The turquoise water swirled around her and she let her mind wander and swirl as well. If she was being honest, which she was scared to do, she felt a few reservations herself. She was quick to dismiss these thoughts as likely hormones. She wondered if there were ever times, in all of history, when a woman gave birth and ended up hating her child. Statistically this has to be true, but it felt like blasphemy to say it out loud.

She had wanted to be a mother and had chosen to try to get pregnant. But now that it was a reality and not some far off hypothetical future, she began to worry. What if she had been conditioned, by society and movies and all that, to want to be a mom? Or maybe 'want' was even the wrong word. Maybe it was more, to believe that was the inevitable next step of life. She was starting to think about all the time and money it would really and truly take to raise a child, and what if James didn't get into it? What if all or the majority of the burden fell to her? She wasn't going to have much of a life of her own for at least the next couple of years and really, much longer than that. Would it all be worth it? What if her child grew up and hated her? Or hated their own life? What if they felt she had taught them wrong, loved them wrong, and blamed her for their dead-end life? And what if it was true? Maybe she wouldn't rise to the occasion. Or maybe she would do her absolute best and her child would still grow up in this sometimes-shitty world and feel the crush of existential dread like we all do. For some of us it crushes us completely.

It was all a little overwhelming when she thought about it too much. Better to not think, just soak for a few minutes while the water was still warm and delicious around her. She shifted gingerly and felt a sharp pain in her side. It felt like a stitch, as if she had been running and had winded herself, which she would do if she ever ran. She instinctively pressed her hand to her side, as if pushing things back in place. The pain did not stop. In fact, it deepened. Ela decided to get out of tub. She placed one hand on each side, bracing herself so she wouldn't slip. She knocked her phone off the edge, it went skittering across the tiled floor under the cabinet. She hoped she hadn't cracked it, but barely had time to register the thought when another wave of pain cut through her side. It felt as if her intestines where ripping apart. Was this what a contraction felt like? But it was far too soon for those.

She placed one foot over the edge of the tub, down onto the worn and familiar bathmat she'd owned since college. It was shaped like a half daisy and used to be white and orange but was beige and gray these days. That's when she noticed the blood. It trickled from her ankle onto one beige daisy petal. She gasped. When Ela looked down, her other foot still being in the tub, the water was a black crimson. Deep red mixed with the turquoise bath bomb made the water look menacing. With her side still splitting in pain, Ela quickly got down on all fours to reach for her phone under the cabinet. Should she call James or just dial 911? Was this an emergency? She'd never called 911 before. Somehow, she knew, deep down, this was the beginning of the end. She was having a miscarriage. She began to cry, and she didn't know if it was fear, pain, grief, or relief. It was a mixture of all, swirled together in a nasty concoction inside her heart that mirrored the mess inside her tub. She finally reached the phone and dialed 911, laying on the cold tile floor which was now covered in her own blood.

She had not been prepared for this. Miscarriage wasn't something anyone really prepares you for, only some footnote warnings in the pamphlets the doctors give out at early visits. She found out what it feels like to have your baby die inside you. It was different than she would have guessed. She would have guessed it would feel like your life is over, but it didn't. Instead it felt more like being frozen. Stuck in an endless ice sculpture of pain, shame, and longing. And for her, a tinge of relief here and there that she pushed away quickly, hating herself that it was there. It seemed like it hit James much worse. He actually seemed to mourn. Which was the first time she felt 100% that he did in fact want to be a father. How tragic that it was only once he certainly wasn't.

The second thing that happens after your baby dies is everyone else just keeps on living. She watched through her icy cage. At first, needing to stay in bed to recover, she mostly watched the world go on through the tiny window of her phone's screen as she scrolled social media. People continued to get married, get new jobs, buy houses, and they even had the audacity to get pregnant and have their own babies. Even mundane holidays were now awful as she had to see a million photos of kids playing with sparklers on July fourth, or opening Easter baskets in April. The first days of school were a time she felt she had to look away and every kid held up a chalkboard on their front porch proudly displaying what grade they were going into and what they wanted to be when they grew up. They would celebrate, as if no one else in the world could possibly be suffering through the exact opposite and watching. It felt like torture, but she also had a hard time looking away, like a car crash. She had to come to terms with the fact that she was the loser. She lost her child. Which made them the winners. They won, she lost.

She also began to slowly realize there was another thing they don't prepare you for when your baby dies: The reminders. Fucking everything reminded her. Constantly. There was the first wave. She and James came home from the hospital after recovering. On the drive home there was an empty car seat in the back, that was bought with the intention of holding a shrieking infant eventually. She had bought it perhaps too early, but she had wanted to practice putting the baby in and taking it out as she'd heard it was difficult. Now she didn't even consider throwing it away, how could she? Would they try again? How could she even begin to think about that? She walked into their little yellow bungalow and headed toward their bedroom, James unloading the car. Before Ela could make it, she passed her most recent home project, the nursery. The crib sat in the corner, just a cage without a lid. There were toys no one would ever play with, books she would never read to anyone as they fall asleep, and so many diapers that would never be used. She sat in the rocking chair, and rocked. "At least the rocking chair is getting used," she thought. Ela didn't even realize she was crying until James materialized at her side and took her hand. She felt the top edge of the collar of her shirt damp against her skin. She must have been crying for a while.

After, he tucked her into bed, pulling the covers up to her shoulders. It wasn't even cold. "Is this what he would have done to their child?" she wondered. "Suffocate it in bed sheets? Jesus." She wasn't sleepy, but she didn't want to do anything and certainly didn't want to think. So she pulled out her phone and scrolled. She lost count of how many days and nights she got through this way.

She had started following a bunch of sugar cookie accounts years ago when she got into baking. A short-lived stint. This led her to become familiar with food bloggers, which led to home bloggers, then fashion bloggers, and so on. Although not everyone blogs, they mostly post to Instagram. They are influencers. She followed along, liking and commenting sometimes but mostly watching. After her baby died, Ela lived most of her waking life on her phone—a great way to kill hours of time. She thought of starting a fresh account, something not personal. She didn't have much going on in her personal life she wanted to share. But what would she share? The whole thing felt overwhelming. Too much work. Scrolling was easier.

Eventually the lights outside their window grew dark, James came to bed and turned off the wall sconce. The only light left in their little room was her bright phone screen, which she held too close to her face, still scrolling. Not really even reading anymore, just scrolling for the colors and the company.

Ela knew she should go to therapy, find God, pick herself up by her bootstraps, take up running marathons, make big goals, or whatever else people tell you to do when you're in the middle of everything falling apart. She didn't do any of those things. They struck her as desperate and stupid.

Ela stayed frozen for months. Mostly scrolling, not eating, hating everything but mostly hating herself. She lost a lot of weight, which was easy since everything tasted like ash in her mouth. She began to suspect she lost so much weight because she was trying to starve her body, punishing it for losing her baby. This body she lived in was a murderer, and her savior; a messy tangled mess that she felt no love for.

There were times she felt a little better. She would shower, eat some toast. Maybe sew something in her studio. But then she'd walk past the nursery, looking exactly how it looked when they had first put everything together, so full of expectation and hope. And she would remember. And she would get back in bed. The warmth of the sheets enclosing her like a womb, like a tomb. *How fitting these two words were so similar,* she thought.

Eventually they shut the nursery door and never opened it. She and James didn't discuss this, it was just a silent agreement they came to. They came to a lot of silent agreements during this time but this one was by far the most useful. That door led nowhere so they never opened it.

Then Ela would have another good week. She started thinking about going back to work. And then a holiday would come. Here's what she quickly discovered about holidays on Instagram: they are landmines waiting to be stepped on by someone like her. They are full of little kids doing cute things, making memories and their moms capturing it on camera for the world to see. She would never capture her child doing anything, no fireworks or tooth fairy visits or first day of school pictures by the front door. She would watch all the influencers she followed celebrating the lives of their children and their beautiful, picture-perfect families and a mixture of jealousy, envy and dismissal would grow and fester inside her heart.

James tried to encourage her to avoid social media. But she had every right to be on there. They were posting for her to see, presumably. The problem was them and their inability to consider others. If anyone should stop being on Instagram it was them, not her. She had already had a couple fights with James over it. From her perspective he seemed to take their side, saying she was getting too caught up in the online world anyway. And she felt it was more a matter of justice and, frankly, consideration. If they were going to be online, making money off their audience, then they chose to put their lives out there and therefore they needed to learn how to behave with their audience in mind and not just themselves. She'd tried leaving comments or even private direct messages, but more often than not all this would result in was her getting blocked. When she'd check the accounts from her laptop (which wasn't blocked if she didn't log in), she could see no change in their behavior. They learned nothing. They just ignored her. Something bigger needed to be done. Something that made them see her point of view. And it was going to be up to her to do it. She was going to need to be the change she wanted to see in the world.

CHAPTER 3

Rosie
@bedofrosies

2,569 POSTS | **237K** FOLLOWERS | **788** FOLLOWING

Rosie turned her ring light on before the Zoom call started. And thank GOD because she had a melted chocolate chip resting above her upper lip like a cartoon Hitler. Or Charlie Chaplin, but when you see a tiny mustache no one thinks of Charlie first. Rosie had learned that her shaded home office was not the most flattering light in her house, which was why she used her ring light. Working from home for the past couple of years had changed her. Now she only got dressed and put makeup on if she was shooting content or if she had a RTLAS call. Otherwise it was yoga pants and messy bun day, again. She had vowed it wouldn't get this way, but it had. It was sort of liberating to be cliché sometimes.

The other RTLAS women, which stood for Rising Tide Lifts All Ships, were fellow influencers she respected. They had all made content creation their full-time jobs for years now and they had decided to meet once a month over Zoom to share notes and offer whatever they could to help one another. It made Rosie feel less alone. She loved the freedom and independence of working for herself, but she missed having coworkers. The RTLAS group was a breath of fresh air; women who spoke the same language. Although they were actually all quite different, it was truly so helpful to be able to talk to other women who did the same thing she did. Even though she hadn't met them all IRL, only Carmen who had been in town once last year for an event, they had already formed a special connection. It felt like they had their own language, or short-hand they could use when talking. They didn't have to over-explain everything, like she did with other friends who sometimes didn't even know what being an influencer was. If Rosie had a dollar for every time someone had said, 'oh, you can make money at that?' over the years she'd have at least fifty dollars. Too bad you can't monetize annoying questions. It was also great to have a group where she could discuss internet troll comments, or annoying things brands did, like try to pay you in product instead of money, and not have to immediately back it up with a mini speech about how grateful you were. Of course she was grateful. Was it only true if she said it publicly every single day? It was nice having, well, basically a support group.

Her laptop pinged loudly as the other members joined the group call. There was Abby, who was always first to the call as well as the first to leave. She almost always had something after, usually school pick up for her son. Even though Abby was in LA, two hours behind Rosie's Kansas City time zone, she still was always hopping off calls first. Next Leena's dark-complexioned face popped onto the screen, she smiled shyly while clearly clicking her unmute button. Leena was newer to the group, like Rosie. She was based in Houston and her account mainly focused on Indian dishes, many of them family recipes as well as new takes on classics. And of course, Carmen was late again.

The dots indicating Carmen was typing popped up at the bottom of their screens.

"Finishing another call. Start without me," it read. The three women stared at one another through their computer screens.

"Well, I guess we can start without her then." Abby said tentatively. "Who wants to go first?"

"I'll start." Leena said, after a longer than necessary pause. Clearly Rosie and Abby had been on the same wave-length and had been prepared to wait her out. Leena never started without a little nudge.

"I had an interesting offer last week. I was approached by Native Forest for a three-post series. They do a number of products, but I'm hoping to pitch them on mostly recipes that involve their organic coconut milk. It feels like a natural fit, although I wish the fee were higher."

Abby and Rosie silently stared back, leaving a long pause.

"I guess I never know if I should say exact numbers in this group. Is that OK? I know we have different size accounts and work in different areas so, I don't know, I don't want to make anything weird," Leena said.

A loud ping erupted from Rosie's laptop.

"Who's making it weird?! At least wait for me!" Carmen said as she entered the group call, laughing at her own joke.

"Leena is considering a three-post campaign with a coconut milk brand. But she's not sure the money is worth it," Abby summarized.

"Well what did they offer?" Carmen asked bluntly.

"It's $6,000 for the three posts," Leena said, her eyes darting away as she did.

"Will the blog posts, recipes I'm assuming, get promoted on Instagram or Pinterest? Maybe you could offer to add that for a little bit more, or just keep it as only blog posts for their proposed $6,000.

Make sure to highlight your stats on both those channels if you pitch that, I know your stuff does great on Pinterest especially," Rosie offered with an encouraging smile.

"Yeah. That seems fair," Leena said. Clearly mulling it over. It was hard to imagine Leena asking for more money, but Rosie knew she must do it from time to time. They all did, it was part of the job. When you are a freelancer, you advocate for yourself or no one does, as Carmen always liked to remind the group.

Abby and Carmen talked through their latest offers, unpaid invoices, and other misadventures while everyone tried to offer up solutions or, at the very least, a bit of empathy for when work didn't pan out. Carmen also talked about an event she was hoping to get booked for in Houston, although it was still far out. She asked Leena if they could meet up, since she was the last one in the group Carmen hadn't met in real life yet. Leena immediately offered her guest bedroom, it was that kind of group. Rosie deliberately waited to go last this time, she had some news beyond just work to share. Finally, it was her turn.

"Rosie, I'm sorry, but I'll have to hop off in ten minutes. I just want to say that before you start because it feels slightly less rude that way. But only slightly." Abby said.

"I figured. It's cool. I'll start with the big news first then," Rosie said. She let out a big sigh, realizing this was the first time she had told anyone other than her husband and her parents. She could feel the group's eyes widen from the little windows on her screen, everyone could feel the anticipation.

"I'm pregnant!" Before she could get another sentence out she heard cheers and claps erupt from her laptop. A wide smile crossed over her face, and she could feel the heat of blush forming at her cheeks.

"We've been trying for a little while now and it's still really early. Just a little over two months. Obviously, I don't plan to announce anything online until at least 12 weeks, but I'll probably wait longer," Rosie continued.

"How come? You just don't feel ready? Obviously, no pressure but I am sure your audience is going to be as thrilled for you as we are," Carmen said. Rosie met Abby's eyes across the screens and she could tell Abby already knew exactly what she was going to say. Carmen had declared herself as the designated cool aunt of the community, she seemed not interested, at least not now, in becoming a mother so it wasn't surprising to Rosie that Carmen might not know some of the logistics.

"Well, actually it's more that I'm waiting for my chances of a miscarriage to go down some. They are the highest in the first trimester," Rosie explained.

"Oh! I actually didn't know that. Makes sense," Carmen said.

"Yeah, I read once that there's something like a 20-25% chance of miscarriage in the first three months," Leena chimed in.

"It feels higher in our community to me," Abby said. "Maybe it's just because some choose to be more vocal about it, when they go through it. I love that we talk about it more than women did in past generations, but to me it also makes it feel more likely in a way. If that even makes sense. Maybe that's just superstitious."

"That's kind of how I feel too. And although I love that other influencers choose to share that journey, I don't think I'll want to if I go through that," Rosie said. "I think I'd rather go through the grief more privately, with my family and close friends. So, that's part of why I may wait a little longer before I say anything online."

"Well, I am so, so happy for you. We all are! And I'm sorry I have to hop off now but do hit me up if you want any tips on mommy campaigns you could pursue if you're going that route," Abby said with a wink. The group laughed and said their quick goodbyes to Abby before her video window went dark and closed out.

Rosie continued her update, which was short. She was already starting to make some space in her sponsorships calendar for around the time she would deliver. And she had already had to turn down one alcohol brand that she loved and had wanted to work with for years. She begged them to keep her in mind for the following year. Carmen suggested she go ahead and pitch them something for next holiday season, just so they could really see her interest.

"Oh, I forgot to add this to my update!" Carmen exclaimed as the call was drawing to a close. "I'm going to be interviewed by Joan Everwood."

"Really? The podcaster?" Leena asked.

Rosie chimed in with her best impression, "I'm Joan Everwood. And you're listening to *This Is Now.*" Which actually sounded a lot like her.

"Yeah. I'm excited! I guess she's working on some story about the influencer community. I don't know much more about it than that. I kind of got the impression that she might not totally know what the story's about yet either. Like it's in the beginning stages. So, who even knows if anything will come of it. But, I'm such a big fan of her podcast that I literally gasped when I saw her email," Carmen explained.

"Well, if she needs any other influencers to interview, throw my name in for sure. I love that show!" Rosie said.

"Did you get the sense it was, I don't know, like a real take on the industry?" Leena asked tentatively.

"I did. I don't think it's a smear piece. Or that Joan thinks all influencers are just vapid narcissists, although we all know a few of those in the community so who can blame her if she did? I think since she has a podcast she's a lot more aware of new media generally than someone with only a traditional background. Or at least that was my take from her admittedly short email."

"I love her show, so I'm sure it'll be a great piece. I just get sick of getting the same questions in interviews sometimes. You know?" Leena asked.

"Oh, you mean like 'How do you actually make money at that?' or 'Do brands really pay you to talk about their products?' As if they've never seen a commercial or advertisement in their life," Carmen chuckled.

"Well, Carmen, everyone knows magazines are a real industry, but blogs are just things your bored aunt writes in her free time," Rosie joked.

"This bored aunt makes six figures a year!" Carmen declared, and the group erupted in laughter. This was the shorthand that Rosie cherished most.

The call came to an end, although all the women lingered longer than they really needed to. Rosie almost wished they talked more often than once a month, although there were tons and tons of texts and Instagram DMs exchanged in between. It had felt really good to tell a few friends about the pregnancy too. It made it feel more real. Even though she'd already started her doctor's appointments, and she knew she was in fact pregnant, so far it was a little hard to believe as the only symptom was some nausea in the mornings and the disappearance of her period. She was thinking about telling her friend Jackie, who was herself an OB/GYN and would understand her reasons for privacy and would give her space or support if a miscarriage happened. Maybe she was overthinking the miscarriage thing. But, it was true that it felt like influencers had even higher rates, although it was probably just that they more openly talked about it. She wasn't a superstitious person usually, but she didn't want to jinx anything.

She also had her own internal doubts about it all. What if she hated motherhood, or worse, didn't bond with her child once they were born? So far, she didn't really feel any connection to the collection of cells that was rapidly forming inside her, but maybe that was normal? She had wanted to be a mom, and it felt like the next logical step in her life and in her marriage. But still she worried. Doing new things was always terrifying and the internet was not a kind place to new moms, she had seen.

Her phone buzzed on her desk and she saw her husband's name pop up.

> What about Franklin, or Franklyn, for a girl?
> We could call her Frankie.

She smiled. He was thinking about their child at the same time as her. Cliché she supposed, but she felt reassured. It felt good to not be so alone in all the newness. Which made her think about single moms and what they must go through. She would have to make a point to be more supportive of single moms she knew or met in the future, because geez that looked even harder than she'd realized before.

She texted back:

> I like Frankie.

And as the text went out across the internet to her husband's phone, she placed her hand across her stomach and tried to imagine what it would feel like in a few months once it was rounded and full. She smiled. She decided to go ahead and send a quick text to her friend Jackie to see when they could hang out next, as Jackie's doctor schedule was infinitely busier than her own.

> Would love to see you sometime soon. I have some news.

She typed. She knew it could be several minutes or hours before she heard back, especially if Jackie was at work. So, she was surprised to see the little typing dots pop up on her screen.

> Me too! Could you come to the hospital for a quick lunch next week? My schedule is so nuts rn that would be easiest for me.

Jackie texted back. Rosie always appreciated they had the kind of relationship where Jackie felt OK to offer up fairly lame hangs such as this, just so the two could connect. It meant she really did want to see Rosie, even though her life was clearly very full.

> Actually, here's my news. I'm too excited to wait...

Jackie wrote. Then the next line, in all caps with a bunch of confetti emojis read:

> I'M PREGNANT!

Rosie gasped and dropped her phone, and it made a muted plop on her rug below.

CHAPTER 4

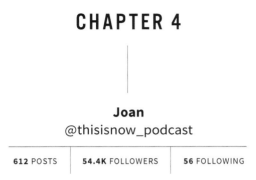

Joan
@thisisnow_podcast

612 POSTS | **54.4K** FOLLOWERS | **56** FOLLOWING

J oan clicked to begin saving out her audio file, removing her head-phones as she watched the progress bar begin to scroll ever so slowly. She really needed to invest in a new laptop sooner than later, but she hated moving everything over and resaving all her passwords (likely forgetting some in the process). She gently pushed her right leg forward, the creaking bifold closet door folding out, letting more light into the closet. Joan heard something in her knees pop as she ex-tracted herself from the cushion where she'd been sitting on the floor. They'd moved in over a month ago, but she still hadn't made time to set up a proper recording space. So far, their bedroom closet had proved to be the best, most acoustic option. And she always tried to make sure the audio for the recorded ads sounded as clean as possible; she hated to get notes from advertisers asking her to do them again. Recording the ads for her podcast, *This Is Now*, was easily her least favorite part of the job. It felt so contrary to everything she'd learned as a journalism major, although that was many years ago. She was grateful for the freedom hosting her own podcast had brought and she knew ads were part of it. It didn't make money solely from having listeners, that's just not how things worked in the podcast world (or even at NPR where she'd interned before going freelance). It was a necessary evil and really, it wasn't all that evil or all that difficult. But still, she hated lending her voice to selling hair dye or meal planning kits. It was all a little surreal.

While the progress bar continued, Joan cleaned up her makeshift studio—which mostly involved putting cushions back on their bed and putting away all the wires and extension cords she had to use in order to record in her closet. She liked to have everything put away before her partner got home. Monica never minded a mess, but Joan did. And she felt that if she left a mess for Monica to see then it would only encourage more messes. So far, the house had stayed relatively clean, minus a few boxes they still needed to unpack. They had finally made the move from New York to Los Angeles, well, Pasadena to be more accurate. They both had been craving a change for a few years and wanted a space with a little more room than their NYC studio apartment had offered. Thanks to the success of *This Is Now*, they had been able to take the leap.

She made a quick snack of Greek yogurt with honey and granola, which she ate as she jotted a few notes. She was one of those people who still preferred to write things in notebooks, it just felt so much faster than thumbing out notes on her phone. She only had about 20 minutes before she should probably leave to meet Carmen. And the truth was she wasn't prepared at all. They had made plans to grab an afternoon coffee, just to explore some ideas, and Joan had assured her she wasn't planning to record the conversation. She really didn't even know what she wanted the story to be, she just felt that doing something on influencers was relevant. And since *This Is Now* was mostly a blend of pop culture, current events, and modern-day crime stories, not to mention a listenership of mostly women for whatever reason, she had a hunch there was a story there that would resonate. She just didn't know what yet. As she quickly chewed she added to her notes, which read:

- Gig culture, working for yourself
- Being a woman on the internet / social media
- Trolls / cancel culture, navigating (too trod?)
- Connecting personally online
- Safety and privacy while sharing online

Even she was bored looking at her list. She knew she didn't have it yet. But she was hoping that by making a few connections with people who had made a career out of being an influencer, she could scratch past the surface and find the real story that would capture her as well as her listeners' imagination. Joan was nothing if not curious. She just hoped Carmen wouldn't feel the meeting was a waste of her time since Joan clearly didn't have a direction yet.

Carmen walked down the hill from her house, already regretting her choice of wedge espadrille sandals. She had suggested to Joan they meet at Moon Juice for a coffee, although she realized later it was more a juice / alternative milk joint and she just hoped they did in fact have lattes or something. She actually wasn't sure. But who didn't like expensive juice?

She pulled the glass door open and was immediately hit with the scent of herbs, earth, and coffee. They must at least have an espresso machine, although she'd never bothered to look before. Half of what she loved about the place was the décor. It was all rounded corners and muted warm tones; pinks, reds, and browns. The whole place felt like a chic cave or something. She pulled her red leather wallet out as she approached the counter, ordering a bottled alternative milk option, which was a silky blue color and literally shimmered somehow, and a no-dairy grain-free cookie. She was sure the cookie would suck but it was something to chew. This was a very LA milk and cookie situation, she chuckled to herself. As she picked up her order she scanned the room for a place to sit, although the shop had very limited seating. It was mostly a take-away counter. This truly had been a poor suggestion, she was realizing.

Just then she saw Joan enter the shop. Carmen had googled her image since she was mostly more familiar with her voice than what she looked like. She had been surprised to find that Joan had long sandy blonde hair and a warm, inviting face (just like her voice). She had been expecting a cropped cut and cute journalism glasses, kind of a Terry Gross look. A strange assumption once she realized it. Carmen figured Joan knew what she looked like, given how visible she was online. But she never acted like she assumed people knew who she was, even if she could tell they did. It was just too stuck-up seeming to her. She waved across the room and caught Joan's eye as she headed over.

"Hi! I'm Carmen. You must be Joan."

"Yes, hello. Thank you again for meeting me," Joan said as began to reach out to shake Carmen's hand. Carmen didn't notice and immediately pulled her into a hug, pressing her cold bottled milk into Joan's back for one shocking instant.

"So, this may have been poor suggestion on my part," Carmen blurted.

"Oh?" Joan scanned the shop, clearly not seeing anything wrong.

"They don't have coffee, just weird lattes. And I'm not sure we can get a seat, as there aren't many. I don't live far so if you'd like to get something to go, we could walk to my house. I'm sure you can leave your car in the parking lot for at least an hour or so," she suggested.

"I don't mind a weird latte,' Joan said, with a mischievous smile.

"Good. Then you'll love it. This is a milk," Carmen laughed, holding up her blue concoction. She could see the gal behind the counter roll her eyes at them ever so subtly. Carmen couldn't help but make a small scene (or a big scene) nearly everywhere she went. Joan scanned the menu and ordered a galaxy latte. Once she had her order in hand, the two women exited the shop and Carmen led the way up the hill to her house.

"This is a really cute neighborhood," Joan commented as they waved to a woman walking past, pushing a sleek modern-looking stroller.

"Yeah, thanks. I've lived in Silver Lake almost three years now. Before that I had a place in Korea Town, which was cute too but in a very different way. I like it here. It actually feels very chill and almost small town for LA."

"We just moved to Pasadena. I was in New York before, in Brooklyn. It could not feel more different but we're liking it so far. I'm still getting used to driving again though."

"Driving is the worst part, I think. But you can't beat the weather. I know that's SUCH a cliché but it's true," Carmen laughed.

The two arrived outside Carmen's house, which was one side of a small but tidy little duplex. She used the keypad to type in her door code and led Joan inside. She hadn't been planning to invite Joan over, so the place was a little less picked up than she would have preferred. Oh well. Why not let the journalist see her pigsty of a home, she thought. Carmen quickly cleared her kitchen table of the breakfast things she'd left out, brushing a few crumbs away while Joan pretended not to notice. They sat down on her vintage rattan chairs and Joan pulled out a small notebook from her bag.

"I'll just be honest with you, I'm not totally sure what this story is about yet," Joan admitted.

Carmen smiled, "I'll be honest too, I know. I kind of picked up on that," which made Joan laugh.

"In your opinion, what is the most interesting part of your job? Or, at the very least, what do other interviewers ask you that you find so boring? I can cross those off my list." Joan smiled.

Carmen thought for a minute, unwrapping her crumbly-looking cookie and offering Joan a bite, which she declined. She wasn't put off by Joan's question, it was just kind of hard to answer. It was difficult knowing what other people would not know or want to know.

"Of course, people often want to know how much money I make. Or generally what influencers charge for promoting sponsored things. But that's fairly obvious. I mean, do listeners want to know how much your podcast charges for your ads?"

"Actually, no. I rarely get asked that kind of thing," Joan admitted. Carmen just shrugged.

"Probably one conversation that I think both people in my industry, and those outside of it, find interesting is around being a public figure and how much, then, the public is owed certain information or certain aspects of your life. If that makes sense? I'm not sure exactly what to call that. But take actual celebrities, instead of influencers, if a movie star gets a DUI or gets caught on tape saying something racist, or even is just going through a nasty divorce or something, the public generally feels they are owed that information. The idea being something like, we as the audience are the reason you make money. We consume your movies, or whatever it is. So, you owe us your life information. And also, if a celebrity, or even an influencer like me, chooses to live a public life. Meaning they choose to put their life online or whatever, then there is often this feeling that person then owes their entire life's info to the public. The public is allowed to demand to know anything or everything, or get access like photos of private moments."

"Yes. It's not new, just a new nuance to the conversation we've been having a long time. I know this was a big topic after Lady Diana died. The sentiment that if the public hadn't been so demanding of photos of her private life maybe her car accident wouldn't have happened. That kind of thing?"

"Exactly! Although I hope you know I am in no way comparing myself to a celebrity or, god, to someone as famous as Diana," Carmen laughed. "I'm self-absorbed but not that self-absorbed."

"We're all self-absorbed," Joan reassured her. And Carmen felt it was genuine, which really made her feel that Joan was not there to get some kind of scoop or potentially take a few shots at their online community. She felt Joan really got it. She was genuinely curious and wanted to tell something truthful with heart in her story. Carmen only hoped she could help.

"And do you agree? Do you think because you've chosen to lead a public life you owe the public your life's story or however you would describe it?" Joan asked.

Carmen thought, taking a sip of her blue milk drink. She made a face.

"This tastes like leaves, basically the opposite of how it looks. I regret my choice." And Carmen was delighted Joan suppressed a laugh. "OK, so I both agree and disagree. I do think if you chose to live online then, well, you chose that, and you should be aware there may be consequences at times that you don't love. Or, maybe that's too harsh. I just mean there is a relationship there, between you and your audience, and good relationships are never one sided," Carmen said. "That being said, I also think you are allowed to set boundaries. Just because I post photos of my outfits doesn't mean I have to show you my dirty laundry, you know? I think people can ask whatever they want, but you should be allowed to not answer."

"Mm. That makes sense to me. I'm just going to jot a couple notes," Joan said as she scribbled a few things in her small notebook.

"This is switching gears, but it's related. There is also this conversation I see pretty often where the audience kind of acts entitled to be able to be a part of your story. Maybe that's confusing, let me think of an example," Carmen took another sip of her terrible drink as she tried to sort through her thoughts. She hoped she was making some sense.

"Oh! I know. One I see often is when influencers announce they are pregnant. If they have a decent size following you'll see at least a few comments about how they did their announcement wrong because they weren't sensitive enough to people who want to have children but can't, people who have gone through miscarriage, and people who maybe don't want children at all. Personally, I don't really want children. At least that's how I feel right now. But it makes no sense to me why I would be annoyed with someone who clearly does want children and announces this happy news in their life. You know?" Carmen could tell she was being a little all over the place with her thoughts. Hopefully that was something Joan was used to, given she was clearly a professional interviewer and probably used to people's random brain connections. Or at least Carmen hoped.

"Yes, I think I know what you're saying. The audience is there, presumably, because they want to hear about you. But then if you share something about you that the audience feels triggered by or feels you didn't consider them enough in your news about yourself, there is some hurt there. That was the least concise way of saying it, I'm sure," Joan said with a smile.

"No, that's exactly it. And to be fair, I do think when you are talking to a larger group of people, like online, it is good practice to be considerate of this fact. But, I also think, it's impossible to share your own authentic truth without it being very much about you. Since you can't have the experience of a large group. You are only you, after all."

"Does this type of thing mostly happen around pregnancy announcements?" Joan asked.

"I think that's the biggest and loudest one I see. Probably because so many of the audiences I deal in are mostly made up of women, and whether you choose to have children or not is such a big question in women's lives in ways I'm not sure men have to deal with on the same level. I think there is just a lot there that can be triggered. I sort of hate that word actually."

"Triggered?"

"Yes. And also, when people say, 'trigger warning.' But, I totally appreciate the thought behind it. It's just kind of overused. But maybe I'm being uncharitable?" Carmen said. She could feel she was getting too comfortable with Joan, which she liked. But she didn't want to come off unkind.

"I think it's a little overused too," Joan said with a small smile. "I probably should walk back to my car soon. So far LA feels like a very parking ticket obsessed city. Is there anything else you feel like you want to share with me? No pressure."

"Well, I feel hesitant on this one. Again, I feel so random throwing a bunch of barely connected thoughts at you," Carmen confessed.

"Please, throw it."

"OK, so I don't have any studies to cite. But it seems to me there is a growing conversation around how the internet, and specifically social media, impacts mental health. I think a lot of it is currently focused on kids, or teenagers. And I think it should be focused there first of course. But I do wonder about its impact on adults. It seems like it can't be all that good, I mean from a macro like how it affects the whole US or something along those lines. Obviously every individual has their own relationship to it."

Joan considered this, "So, the thing you've made your career on, you're concerned it's bad for people?"

"Yes. And I know a lot of my friends who do this kind of work worry about it. We also feel a lot of those negative effects since being good at being online means you kind of have to be online a lot. I guess I'm worried I'm a snake eating its tail, and maybe my career hurts people more than it helps. I don't want to be the villain. No one ever thinks they are, right?" Carmen was trying to lighten this admission. But she did feel guilt about it and she knew Joan could tell. Carmen was always an open book.

The conversation came to a natural close and Carmen rose to walk Joan to her front door.

"I'd love to talk again sometime if you're open to it? You gave me a lot to think on, as I explore a story idea. Actually, and this is a bit forward so do know you can say no, I'd love to go to an event where there are other influencers or potentially meet a few other people you know who are doing what you do. It always feels like when I meet people though others they feel less distrustful of my intentions," Joan said.

"Totally. I get that. And yeah, let's talk again. Or if there's something that comes up that I think might be interesting for you I'll let you know," Carmen said, holding the door and letting sunshine stream into her small entryway.

"Thank you. Really." Joan smiled and then turned to walk back down the hill toward the coffee shop. She had no idea this short conversation was going to change the trajectory of her career.

CHAPTER 5

Pam
@freshlystitched

| **148** POSTS | **32K** FOLLOWERS | **2,591** FOLLOWING |

F eeling some semblance of peace for the first time in years, Pam finished watering her plants as the late afternoon sun streamed in through her porch windows. She had accumulated a lot of plants over the years; it was like a miniature greenhouse at this point. Her favorites were the thriving split leaf plants (Monstera deliciosa) that snaked around the room, climbing the stakes she had planted in their pots and onto the walls. Normally a plant that thrived in the tropics, she had managed to create an atmosphere they seemed to love right here in her Columbia, Missouri home. Smack in the middle of the country and about as far from a tropical climate as you could get.

She had recently found a few stained glass panels at a flea market and hung them up in front of the porch windows, which was really more like a sunroom. She felt pretty confident the panels had belonged to a church at some point; there were depictions of Mary holding baby Jesus with rays of rainbows shooting out in all directions. Pam wasn't religious, but she absolutely loved the way the colors splashed across her plant room this time of day, which was why she had left the watering until now. The room was filled with bright swatches of red, orange, green and blue. It felt almost surreal, a little trippy.

Pam had enjoyed her three-day weekend, although she was looking forward to returning to the nursery tomorrow. She missed her work plants, even as she tended to her house plants. She had spent most of her long weekend at home, working on some commission pieces as well as updating a few things on her blog. Really, she should figure out how to photograph her plant room when the stain glass was all lit up for her blog. As she thought about it she also realized the image would probably perform really well on Instagram too. She decided to give it a try, so she moved a few plants around and removed some of the clutter of her watering can and gardening gloves. Then she stood back and snapped a few pictures on her phone, contorting her body to get different angles. She'd edit one later and maybe put it up if she felt it was good enough. The hardest part was coming up with captions. She never felt like she had anything important to say; her life was so mundane.

She walked into her kitchen and checked the oven clock. It read 4:48. Close enough. She opened a bottle of wine and poured herself a glass. She owned a set of fancy wine glasses but usually she preferred to use recycled jars instead, the same ones she used for water. She had recently made a pact with herself to not start drinking until after 5:00, which it basically was now. She pressed the button to start preheating the oven and pulled a frozen pizza box from the freezer drawer. *Another fancy night alone,* she thought and laughed at herself. She sat on the counter as she waited for the oven to warm up, automatically pulling out her phone as she did.

The photo of the plant room had turned out really pretty if not a little dark. She used her favorite app to bump up the brightness and saturation of the colors. Yes, this was a good one, she thought and smiled. But what should she write for the caption? She took another sip of wine as she thought. Finally, she settled on: 'Feeling recharged this weekend. Ready to go kick Monday's ass tomorrow. Hope you do too!' She nearly jumped as the oven dinged at her, it was ready. She pressed the post button and then set her phone down to unwrap the plastic from around her dinner. Her phone's screen saver started up after only a few seconds. It was a clock, well not a clock so much as a counter. She had the world's population counter always as her phone and computer backdrop. The number ever rising, it was sort of insane. It reminded her how small and insignificant she was, which she found comforting. Her problems weren't that big of a deal; there were millions and millions of other people born every minute with more mundane problems or probably things bigger than hers. She popped the pizza in the oven, then refreshed her wine. She set a timer and settled on the couch to scroll while she waited for her food. Pam had grown a modest online following over the last couple of years, which she mostly felt self-conscious about, but it did help drive sales in her Etsy shop. Which reminded her, she needed to put the commission jackets she'd finished in her car, so she could ship them tomorrow over her lunch. She would pack up the orders after dinner, she decided.

Scrolling down she saw a lot of familiar faces. Everyone posting what they had been doing over the weekend, lots of outdoor family activities. Summer was just coming to a close and she was ready for all the moms she followed to stop complaining about their kids being home all the time. *Not everyone wants to hear about your kids*, she thought. Plus, wasn't complaining about kids you chose to have kind of stupid? But, maybe they couldn't think of what to write for a caption either and that's why they defaulted to. Who knew? Online was a weird place, but it was her second home.

She was still lost in scrolling when her timer flashed across her screen. She headed to the kitchen, taking her glass jar as it was empty again. She noticed her bottle of wine was already nearly half gone. She refilled her glass and thought, *OK no more until after I've eaten a proper meal.* She removed the pizza from the oven, slicing the pie with her giant pizza scissors. They were a menacing sight on her pegboard but very handy. She loved the metallic zing sound they made, while oozing cheese and tomato sauce out the sides of the crust. She had intended to watch something on TV while she ate, but she ended up scrolling for a while longer, sitting under her collection of air plants (Tillandsia) on the couch. Facing the TV but never turning it on.

After Pam cleaned up her few dinner dishes, she poured the remaining wine into the jar; it nearly splashed over. *This is more efficient anyway,* she thought as she tossed the bottle in the recycling. It clinked loudly against other bottles already in the bin. She headed to the bathroom and pulled out a box of touch up dye, her roots had been looking light and dull. She pulled the plastic disposable gloves on and set up what felt like a tiny chemistry lab on her vanity sink. She'd mixed this dye so many times she didn't need the instructions anymore. She stared at herself in her small, oval mirror. Her skin looked dry and tired.

"Mirror, mirror..." she said out loud to her own reflection and then let out a loud cackle as she heard her voice slur slightly. She realized she was pretty buzzed, maybe not the best time to dye your hair. Oh well. She actually hated that she still dyed her roots, it was such a vain activity. Who cared if her new grays began showing, youth was a stupid standard society placed on women. And yet, here she was, touching them up every month.

As she waited for the dye to set, she let her mind wander to the cute new guy at work. He'd only started last week, but she had immediately noticed him. Most of the men who worked at the nursery were more of the rough and tumble type, who you could easily picture lifting heavy plants to place in women's trunks or working outdoors on landscaping. But the new guy, who was so new she hadn't learned his name yet, was probably a few years younger than she was, with a slight build and pale skin. He didn't look like someone who worked outside. In fact, his round Harry-Potter-style glasses made him look more like a plant scientist than anything else. He reminded her a little bit of her ex-husband, but she quickly dismissed the idea, not wanting to be a woman who had a type. It was just a stupid crush anyway.

She was content living alone and being alone after her marriage had completely imploded. She didn't mind being lonely, although she would love to have sex again someday. Probably he thought she was old, or homely. Who knew. Men were mostly stupid and shallow in her experience and she wasn't exactly the supermodel type. Men tended to think they deserved to be with the prettiest woman they could get to fuck them. At least that's what it seemed like her ex had thought, and maybe Pam had been the best he could get when they married but eventually he had been ready to trade up. Or maybe this was the wine talking.

She carefully placed her now half-empty glass on the shower shelf and turned on the tap. She undressed and got in, rinsing out the dye carefully so as not to get it in her eyes. The smell of her mint and lilac soap surrounded her. She went to reach for her glass but the moisture (and perhaps the fact that she was now drunk) made her clumsy and she dropped it. For one terrible moment she watched as the glass jar crashed and shattered inside the tub where she was standing. Tiny shards of glass and red wine sloshing everywhere.

"Fuck!" she yelled. She quickly turned off the water, not wanting the broken glass to go down the drain. She stepped out of the tub, reaching for a towel to wrap around herself. She realized she still had conditioner in her hair. She looked down and saw she had cut one of her toes on the broken glass. A little trail of blood followed her from the tub to the tiled floor. She bent down to see if the glass piece was still lodged in her foot and she nearly toppled over. A vision of herself falling and breaking her neck flashed into her mind's eye. Probably no one would find her dead body for days. And when they did she'd be naked in the bathroom with a broken glass of wine in her tub. *How very, very tragic,* she thought and laughed to herself. Her life truly was hilariously pathetic sometimes.

She lay in bed, under her mass of handmade and vintage quilts; having finally gotten the mess in the bathroom cleaned up and the conditioner out of her hair. She felt exhausted but simultaneously wide-awake, probably from the alcohol. She cursed, and she realized she'd never packed up the orders she needed to mail. Whatever. She'd do it tomorrow.

She rolled on her side and reached for her phone, the light filling up that corner of her bedroom. She checked the likes and comments from her post. Her heart nearly leapt when she saw that Rosie (username: @bedofrosies) had left her a comment. She had written: 'What a beautiful space!' with some plant and flower emojis after. Pam loved Rosie's blog and had followed her account for years. She'd even sent her a gift a few months ago. She did that periodically, partly to network and meet people but also as a way to market her Etsy. She sent things she made, handsewn jackets or prints of her collages among other things. Her shop was a little random but it was all things she passionately made. Pam pressed the heart next to Rosie's comment, even though she knew the activity would not be noticed by someone with an account her size. Still, it was nice to be acknowledged.

CHAPTER 6

Jackie
@docjackie

| **106** POSTS | **330** FOLLOWERS | **452** FOLLOWING |

Her black leather ballet flats squeaked as she walked down the beige linoleum hallway to her office. She gave a quick glance and seeing no one watching her she tugged at her compression tights under her skirt as they had risen up in an uncomfortable way. She had recently begun wearing the compression tights under her usual doctor attire since she was nearing her second trimester and she knew her family history. On days she would be on her feet more, she wore flats with insoles and her compression tights, hoping to avoid some of the more uncomfortable aspects of pregnancy as much as she could.

Even though Jackie was nearing the one third through point she still wasn't showing much. She knew this was normal; she had told many of her patients this very thing over the years. But now that it was her reality, she understood the creeping paranoia one could feel. A big bulging belly, although uncomfortable, was also reassuring that yes, there was a healthy baby in there and you didn't need to worry. Not seeing this outward sign was almost disconcerting, even though Jackie was more aware than most how common and normal it was. She had taken to wearing stretchy pencil skirts most days as they were not only nearly as comfortable as yoga pants (which she obviously could not wear to work) but showed what small belly she had. She rubbed hers now, as she made notes from her last appointment. Her phone buzzed on her desk. A text from Rosie popped up on the screen.

> Just parked. Heading to the cafeteria. See you soon.

Jackie had almost forgotten they had planned to meet for lunch. Life had been far too busy lately. She was grateful for Rosie's flexibility and that she never seemed to resent Jackie's schedule. The two had met years ago, through their husbands, and had quickly become close. Back then Jackie had just been starting her residency while Rosie had started a blog. It had become a running joke between them, how different their career paths were. It was actually a relief at times. To have a close friend with such a different job. At other times though it highlighted the differences between them, making explanations longer and maybe a little tedious. Then Jackie remembered that Rosie had said she had big news. She was glad she'd already shared her own pregnancy news, as she didn't want that to overshadow whatever Rosie had to say. They could just celebrate each other, whatever the news was. Jackie picked up her phone and texted back.

> Just finishing up. Be down in 5.

And then she hurried to type up the rest of her notes before grabbing her purse to head to the elevator.

Rosie awkwardly stood by the end of the cafeteria line. She didn't want to pick out her food until Jackie arrived, in case it took longer than the five minutes Jackie had said. She didn't mind waiting on Jackie or meeting her at the hospital instead of going to a cute lunch spot. She knew it didn't make her a martyr by any means, but it felt nice to be flexible and accommodating to friends. It felt like a small act of love. Plus, Jackie was one of the most intelligent, hilarious, and strong women that Rosie knew. She liked that her life didn't exist online hardly at all. Although sometimes Rosie forgot to update her on major things that she had posted online as she assumed everyone knew. It was kind of self-absorbed to think all your friends saw whatever you post online, but also you could end up repeating information people already knew a lot if you didn't. She had posted about her pregnancy on her account well over a week ago, but she knew Jackie hadn't seen and there was something delightful about getting to tell her IRL.

She saw Jackie emerge from one of the entrances, they caught eyes and Jackie headed her way. Rosie felt weirdly important standing next to Jackie at the hospital, like she was with a VIP or something. The two hugged as they joined the line to get food.

"Thanks for meeting me here again."

"No problem. Honestly the food isn't bad at all. You're probably over it at this point but I kind of like the nostalgia of cafeterias. It's like being in school again."

"Ha! More like being back in institutional life. Like you're visiting me in prison," Jackie quipped.

"Fancy companies like Google have cafeterias on their campuses, not that I've ever been to one. But I've seen photos."

"Yes. It's just like that," Jackie said as she pointedly pulled a not-so-appetizing filet of fish from the warming tray. "It's better than it looks, I swear," she added.

Rosie grabbed the same, she always just ate whatever Jackie ate at the hospital. She assumed Jackie knew better than her what was good.

They paid and then headed to an empty table near the windows. Rosie plopped her purse in an empty chair beside her, not wanting it to sit on the ground. She had another big, brown paper bag with her as well.

"Were you shopping before?" Jackie asked, looking at the bag.

"No. Actually, this is all for you," Rosie picked up the bag and slid it across to Jackie who looked surprised.

"Before you say anything, it's not a gift. Not really anyway. It's all extra things from readers. Things that were sent to me and I just have too much so I'm basically regifting it to you."

"Yes!" Jackie squealed as she pulled out some expensive looking hand lotions. "Finally, some perks of being friends with a celebrity."

"Ha ha. If you're going to mock me I'll just take it back," Rosie joked and she pretended to reach for the bag.

"Oh no you don't. You've already handed me this bag of cast offs, you're not taking it back now. Us commoners have rights, you know. I may only be a doctor, but I deserve…" she paused as she pulled more items from the bag, "…a purple velvet eye mask, not one but two subtly branded baseball caps, and colorful bath bombs. Actually, these do smell amazing. All joking aside, thank you."

"Like I said, it's basically regifting. No thanks needed. It honestly still shocks me how often readers and brands will send me little gifts. It's really sweet but it makes me feel kind of self-conscious, even talking about it to you."

"Well it's working in my favor so keep writing on that blog of yours for sure. This seems like kind of a lot of stuff though, is it always like this?"

"Well no. Actually, this is way more than normal. I announced something recently and that's why I've been getting more stuff. People are just being sweet and celebrating with me. Which is what I wanted to share with you."

"Yes, yes! What's your news?" Jackie asked, taking a big bite of food, and readying herself to listen.

"I'm pregnant, too."

Jackie's jaw opened, a little bite of food spilling out which she quickly wiped away looking sheepish.

"Holy shit Rosie! Oh my god. Now I feel terrible I told you over text. We had the same news?! That's just incredible," Jackie gushed as she scooted up from her side of the table and gave Rosie a little hug. Rosie's eye misted, she was such a crier and even more lately. It felt amazing to have a friend be as excited as she felt herself but rarely showed.

"I just started my second trimester. I thought about telling you sooner, but I was so scared of miscarriage. I mean, I still am, but less so now," Rosie explained.

"Trust me, I get it. I'm so happy for you. And I can't believe we get to do this together! Our little ones can be buds."

"And get ready for endless, shameless texts with questions since you're my only doctor friend. I've tried not to abuse you for free medical advice in the past, but the gloves are coming off now," Rosie teased.

"Do your worst. I will just require more of these cast-off gift bags as payment."

The two friends caught up and laughed about all the gross pregnancy things they'd gone through so far. As Rosie walked to her car in the parking lot after, she could feel she had a big smile on her face. It felt so amazing to talk to Jackie and celebrate together. It made it feel more real; she was actually going to be a mom. She felt her eyes well up again but this time she just let the tears come. Crying in her car had become her main hobby lately; she blamed hormones. She pulled her door shut as she lifted her keys to the ignition, a few more tears rolling down her cheeks. She felt so happy.

Jackie parked her car on the curb outside the house. She could see the realtor, or who she assumed must be their new realtor (they'd only emailed so far) standing just outside the door. She was meeting her husband, to look at the house in person, but he wasn't here yet. She considered waiting in the car, but she could see the realtor was already looking toward where she had parked. Jackie decided to get out, but she wished her husband was there too. She pushed the little fear that nudged at the back of her mind aside.

As she walked up the driveway, toward the front door, the realtor just stared toward her.

"You must be Elise?" Jackie called ahead toward her, "I'm Jackie, nice to finally meet you in real life." She was close enough now that she extended her hand for a handshake. She thought she could see a little surprise in the realtor's eyes but probably she imagined it.

"Oh hi, nice to meet you too," Elise said. Shaking her hand. "Will the doctor be joining us?"

Jackie felt puzzled, but then she quickly realized the mistake. "My husband should be here any minute. We didn't drive together. But, um, I'm the doctor." They both turned as they heard a friendly voice call to them from the street.

"Sorry I'm late. Don't show the house without me."

It was her husband, Paul, still in his nurse's scrubs but he looked every bit the part of a leading man in a romantic comedy. Elise smiled broadly as he approached. Jackie just rolled her eyes. Her husband had this effect on people, which could annoy her but in truth he had this same effect on her. He was charming, and it was genuine. Even if it was annoying how often she didn't get taken seriously unless he was around, or how often people assumed he was the doctor instead of her.

"Well, it's wonderful to meet you both. And I think you're going to love this house even more in person. Shall we?" she gestured for them to enter before her.

And she was right. The house was even better in person. The entryway had a spiral staircase, which although it felt a little outdated it also felt grand. She could imagine a big Christmas tree at the foot of the stairs, their child ripping open presents from beneath it in a few years. Her favorite room was the kitchen. Although she wasn't much of a cook she did love to bake when she had the time. And this kitchen was something straight out of Father of the Bride. It had a big center island, perfect for hosting Thanksgiving with their family one day. Paul seemed to love every feature possible even more than she did, making remarks on their tour. Elise giggled at every single of one his jokes.

"Shall we check out the upstairs? There are four bedrooms, and the previous owner used one as a home office, which you'll see some of their things haven't yet been moved." Elise explained as she ushered them up the winding staircase. They peeked into each room, the main bedroom being the only one that felt distinct. The last one was the home office, a big wooden desk still sitting in the center of the room.

"This one feels like the nursery to me," Paul said. He gently touched Jackie's hand as he did. She saw the happiness in his eyes. Yes, they were ready.

"Oh! Are you expecting?" Elise asked

"Yes, we are. I'm three months along."

"Congratulations! I'm not really supposed to say anything about the schools, but you likely already know the school district here is excellent. In fact, that's why most people move here."

They did know. This was why they were looking here, even though it was a farther drive to the hospital. Jackie just smiled.

"Oh yes, actually I went to school around here. My parents moved once my sister and I left home, but I grew up not too far from here," Paul explained.

Jackie thought about saying she did not. But she wondered if Elise likely already assumed this. Which would annoy her if she did, but also it was true.

"Well then you already know it's a wonderful neighborhood to raise a family in. You're going to love it here."

Jackie would have been annoyed at the presumptive phrasing, as they hadn't signed any contract yet, but she saw the smile in Paul's eyes. He was thrilled. And so was she. She knew they were going to make an offer.

Paul called her as soon as they both pulled away and they talked the whole drive. She was heading home, he was going back to work. They were both so excited. The house would probably be a little more than they had planned to spend, but there wasn't much to fix or renovate so that helped. Jackie wanted to feel settled before the baby arrived. She didn't want to be still packing when her feet swelled, and she could no longer reach her toes. So they might over pay a little, but they decided it would be worth it. She was grateful for a partner to understand her concerns and didn't mind being flexible so she could feel safe. She'd spent so much of her life feeling unsafe, he knew.

Their little historic house was dark when she got home. She made dinner for herself, knowing Paul would be so much later there wasn't much point in making anything for two. She warmed a can of soup, made a salad, added way too many saltine crackers to her soup and listened to her favorite podcast while she ate. The show still had twelve minutes left by the time she was done and had put her dishes in the dishwasher. So, she rummaged through the goodie bag Rosie had given her at lunch. Smelled all the lotions, opened a package of cookies and ate a few. She decided to run a bath and use one of the pretty bath bombs. The water steamed a little as she peeled off her tights and threw the bath bomb in. It was one of those that was full of dried flower petals and little salt crystals and things. It was going to leave a mess in the tub, but she'd worry about that later. Her podcast wrapped up as she pulled up her hair, not wanting to get it wet in the bath. She almost never took baths; this was probably only the third or fourth time she had since they'd moved in together a couple years ago. But something about being pregnant made her want to cradle her body, wrap it up carefully as if it were a baby too. Little did she know this bath would change everything.

CHAPTER 7

Ela
@justanotherela

58 POSTS	**599** FOLLOWERS	**832** FOLLOWING

Six months had passed but Ela barely noticed. She hadn't moved forward or moved on, or whatever you do with grief. James had helped her set up an area for her sewing desk, so there was that. But the only space they really had in their little bungalow was the room that would have been the nursery. So, they had moved the nursery stuff to one side and set up Ela's space on the other. The result? Ela never went in there. It had been such a stupid idea.

She had the sinking suspicion that something was going on with James. They had handled the miscarriage in basically opposite ways. Ela never talked about it, not even really to James. James talked about it endlessly, to anyone who would listen, which Ela knew was probably healthier, but it was also weird. It meant he was always talking about her body while he was standing right by her, talking to other people. Sure, it had been his potential baby too. But it was still weird to hear him talk about body parts he didn't have.

He also had certainly moved on. The event seemed to change something in him, like he grew into a man all in one night. It seemed to solidify in him that he did for sure want children, and soon. Which was not something Ela was ready to talk about yet at all. And he just seemed more serious, and frankly more boring. He started running, he joined a progressive church, which struck Ela as strange and not at all something she wanted to do. She also had this vague sense that he might be seeing someone, maybe someone at work. She couldn't tell if it was her depression and paranoia, but he seemed to be smiling while texting someone a lot more than he used to. They didn't seem like texts with his friends or actual work. He seemed kind of giddy, like he had a crush. She would have checked his phone, but she felt that was beneath her. Plus, she was probably wrong. She wasn't happy, so maybe it just annoyed her to see him smiling all the time, as if nothing had happened.

The worst part was Ela felt completely confused and guilt-ridden. She had wanted a child; she had pushed James to start a family. But once she miscarried, she had felt a mixture of feelings that resembled relief. She was beginning to think that maybe she didn't want children after all. She had just thought that was the next logical step in her life: You finish school. You get a job. You fall in love and get married. You buy a house. You have a child or two.

And then she guessed you got old and waited for them to move out and then you retire from your career. And then you waited to die, probably eating all the pasta you wanted and reading mystery novels along the way. What if she just skipped some of it? What if she just cut to the part where she enjoyed her life now, basically the era she would be in after kids moved out of her home if she'd had any.

But James clearly had different ideas now. She half wondered if she was staying sad and not going back to work or doing anything as an excuse for not being ready to try conceiving again. They had talked about it, she had been honest, but it had just resulted in unresolved fights. And so she had mostly just become unengaged around James, hoping to avoid any further fights. She often waited until around the time he was going to be home from work to go run errands or buy groceries, so she wasn't home when he was. She knew she was just avoiding him, but she needed some space. Then one day he came home early.

James walked into their home an hour earlier than Ela had expected. She was still in her pajamas, and she had just made hot chocolate. James stood across from her in their kitchen, his face sad and serious.

"I want you to be honest with me," he started, "do you want children with me?"

Ela didn't mean to, but she rolled her eyes. She immediately regretted it, she just hated how dramatic he could be. She saw anger flash across his face. She sighed.

"It's not that I don't want to have kids with you. I just don't think I want kids anymore."

"But it was you who wanted to try. What changed? Are you afraid you'll miscarry again?"

"No, it's not that. It's... I don't know how to explain it. It's just like a spell was broken. I realized I don't want to. It's not for me. I'm sorry."

"Thank you for being honest with me," James said. They were both silent for a minute.

"I'm going to be honest with you. I'm not happy in this marriage and I don't think you are either," James said.

"What? What are you talking about? I don't want kids, that doesn't mean I don't want to be married to you," Ela said.

"I've fallen for someone else. And I don't really see a future with us anymore."

"What are you saying? Who?" Ela asked, her voice raising. James just sighed.

"Does it matter? You leave the house before I get home. You roll your eyes at me constantly, you hate when I talk about our baby. You don't want children, I do. And we don't spend time together, ever. I don't even remember the last time we had sex."

"I'm depressed! I'm fucking depressed James, I had a horrible miscarriage and you weren't here! You're over me because I'm sad? Fuck you!" Ela yelled. James didn't respond, he just turned and headed to their bedroom. He started packing a suitcase, filling it with clothes and shoes.

"You can stay in the house, I'll move out," was all he said.

"Who is she? I'm staying in the house because you feel guilty. You fucking cheater," Ela knew she should stop. But she had not seen this coming. She had been suspicious, but this was completely out of left field. She didn't want to have a baby, but she didn't want to be completely alone. How could he leave her now?

To his credit, James didn't yell. He didn't so much as say one mean thing to her as he quickly packed up his suitcase and headed toward the door. Which made Ela even more furious, how could he be so decent about this? He said he was going to go stay at his brother's until he found a new place. And he would let her know when he would come to collect his other things, in case she didn't want to be around. Ela slammed the door behind him, which she also regretted. She put her back against it and slid down, until she was nothing but a puddle on the floor crying.

When they eventually decided to divorce, it felt inevitable, and having no kids and very few assets made it easy. And although Ela was heartbroken, she found that the breakup had the opposite effect on her that the miscarriage had. She went back to her job after only a few months, which had been waiting for her thankfully. She reached out to friends she hadn't really kept up with in years, some got back to her and some didn't. But it was a start. When the sadness felt like it was going to swallow her up, she would go on a walk. Her neighborhood was beautiful this time of year. She made friends with an older man she always saw out on walks, Jim and his dog Lucy. Slowly life began to resemble something she wanted, something she enjoyed.

She continued to be active online, she said so she could keep up with her friends but she followed so many other accounts she rarely saw their posts. Really, she was bored and lonely, she knew. She was scrolling through her feed, mostly full of influencers she liked. All of a sudden James' photo popped up with a young woman, who was clearly flashing her ring finger. The diamond on her ring shone back at Ela through the screen. She dropped her phone, as if it were too hot to hold. The screen cracked, but the photo still looked back at her.

CHAPTER 8

Jackie
@docjackie

106 POSTS	**330** FOLLOWERS	**452** FOLLOWING

S he started to feel strange fifteen minutes into the bath, with the water already beginning to become tepid. At first, she thought it might be heartburn. She'd never actually experienced heartburn before, but she knew that sometimes came on in pregnancies. The slow burn continued to smolder and grow traveling down Jackie's torso as she wrapped her burgundy robe around her waist. The tub was still draining and leaving dried, dead petals and seeds in a ring around the rub. Normally she would have wiped it out, but she felt so uncomfortable the thought of leaning over to clean the tub was unimaginable to her. She decided to lie down and see if that helped.

Jackie stared up at their ceiling fan, willing the pain to lessen. It felt more like a pulsing, throbbing fire deep in her abdomen. She deliberately slowed her breathing, trying not to panic. Something was wrong. Then she felt a hot gush of liquid between her legs, as if her period had just erupted like a volcano. She heard herself cry out, even though no one was there. Doubled over, she awkwardly squatted her way to where she had left her phone, on the dining room table. She could see a trail of blood following her, growing like a long shadow. Her hands shook as she dialed 911.

"911, what's your emergency?"

"I think I'm having a miscarriage. I'm 14 weeks. I have a burning pain in my lower abdomen that just started in the last half hour and I'm bleeding heavily." Jackie heard the last word crack as her throat let out a sob. She told herself to breathe, to list the facts, but she knew this was bad.

"Where are you?" the operator asked. Jackie listed off her address and told the operator she was a doctor and she needed an ambulance right away.

"They are on their way to you now ma'am. Is anyone there with you?"

"No, my husband is at the hospital already. I'm going to sit outside and wait."

"Do you feel faint? Would you like me to stay on the line with you until the ambulance arrives?"

"No. I'm ok." Jackie hung up and grabbed her purse from the table, slowly moving toward the front door. She could feel the blood oozing down her legs and she both wished she wasn't in her robe and also recognized it was probably the most convenient thing she could be wearing for the paramedics. She shut the door behind her but didn't bother locking it, it was too much effort. The pain was searing now, she focused as she sat down on the front stoop. She could already hear sirens somewhere off in the distance, she hoped they were for her. She began to reach for her phone, thinking she would call Paul, but her vision began to darken. She carefully laid her head down on the flower bed soil, not wanting to pass out and crack her head open on the cement. One bloody wound was enough, was her last through before things went dark.

Jackie awoke in the hospital, the familiar sounds and smell greeted her even as she slowly realized she was not there as a doctor. She was the patient in the bed; she was the one hooked up to an IV. She saw Paul sitting in the chair beside her bed, he looked half dead himself. He startled as she smiled at him, as if he had been about to fall asleep.

"Did I lose the baby?"

The expression on Paul's face answered her. She felt her throat tighten, and her eyes began to water. She'd had many patients miscarry over the years, sadly it was all too common. But this immediately felt different. She knew what they had all felt now and it was impossible to really know the pain of this kind of loss until you do.

Paul reached out and held her hand. He was already crying too.

"I'm so glad you're OK. I was so scared for a little bit there that I'd lose you both. I'm so sorry I wasn't home. I wish I had been home," he trailed off.

Jackie squeezed his hand. But she didn't know what to say. She felt too many things all at once. She also felt very tired. Her body couldn't decide if it needed fight, flight, or to go to sleep for a long time.

"Hello Jackie. I wanted to check in, but I can come back?" A young doctor Jackie didn't recognize said. Was this her attending doctor? He must have just finished his residency. His name badge said 'Dr. Claremore' which didn't ring any bells for her. She got the impression though he knew who she was, that she was a doctor here too. She wiped her eyes.

"No, it's ok. Come in. You've already met Paul?" she assumed but asked anyway.

"Yes, he's been with you the whole time, since you arrived."

"What happened? How did I lose it?"

"It's not clear. It's almost like your body had an extreme allergic reaction, possibly to the fetus itself. We also can't rule out genetic or chromosome disorders within the fetus. And that could be why the pregnancy terminated."

Jackie's mind buzzed. Normally her curiosity at such a strange and inconclusive diagnosis would have lit up her mind. But she felt too much sadness, just hearing her baby called a fetus made her want to sob. The young doctor waited, giving her time to process the information.

"I'd like to send the... fetus to pathology. I don't have any family history of any kind of genetic or chromosome condition that I know of. But, I'd like to know more as we do want to start a family."

She could feel Paul tense beside her. No matter the amount of medical training, and they had a lot between the two of them, the thought of their baby being examined was a painful one. This was why most women didn't elect to send a terminated pregnancy to pathology. Even though it could provide more conclusive data that could show whether a healthy pregnancy and baby was possible, Jackie could feel the repulsion too. She didn't want to send the body to the lab, she wanted to bury it and place flowers above the grave and mourn. Not that there was much to bury.

"We can do that. Absolutely," the young doctor replied. He seemed to be waiting for something. But when neither of them offered more he took the cue. "We're going to keep you overnight, we are still waiting on a few more results from the lab. So, get some rest and I'll see you in the morning," he then ducked out the room, closing the door behind him.

Paul met Jackie's eyes, and she immediately fell apart as he rose to hold her.

CHAPTER 9

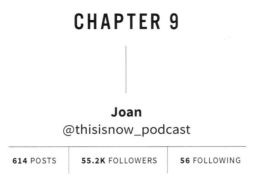

Joan
@thisisnow_podcast

614 POSTS | **55.2K** FOLLOWERS | **56** FOLLOWING

J oan closed her laptop and let out a huff. She could tell ten minutes into the interview that she wouldn't use it. She had kept talking to Pedro for another ten minutes because she didn't want it to be too obvious, as it felt a little rude in the moment. She had learned a few interesting things about the town, maybe that would add color to the final piece. Maybe.

She was trying to put together a follow up episode to her most popular story from the year before, where she had reported on a female serial killer from Iowa. It had been a bizarre and rare case. She hadn't been the one to break the story, but she'd gotten a number of interesting interviews including detectives who had worked on the case. Although Joan really didn't consider herself much of a crime reporter, she was proud how it had turned out. She felt it gave a fuller picture of the story, not reducing it down to good and evil. Life was almost always more complicated than that. And although she had no intention of letting her show turn into a full-on true crime podcast, she wanted to see how the story had impacted the community and those who had known both the killer and victims over the years. But Pedro hadn't known much, or maybe he didn't want to share once he knew the recording had started. It was honestly nuts how much tape she didn't end up using. Most of the time she tried not to think about it. She tried to think of the beginning of her work on a story as sowing seeds, not harvesting a crop. But deadlines always loomed. The content machine must be fed. She jotted that down, maybe something to talk to Carmen about. That must be a challenge she also faced in her job.

Joan carried her laptop into their little kitchen, setting it on top of their worn but beautiful butcher block counters. She clicked on a recipe she had marked, white wine risotto, which she planned to make alongside some simple stir-fried shrimp. Monica wouldn't be home for another hour, so she had plenty of time to throw the dinner together. She opened a chilled bottle of chardonnay and poured herself a glass even though most of the bottle would go into the risotto. She loved slowly cooking a meal while having a glass of wine. Something about it felt very adult to her, so grown up and living in her own romcom. Although life hadn't been much of a romantic comedy lately. She had hoped that the move to sunny LA would feel like a great adventure with Monica, something fresh and exciting between them. But it had mostly felt logistical. Lots of lists, and packing, and unpacking, and rental vans, and lease agreements, and Monica's new work schedule not aligning quite as well with Joan's as it used to. She turned on some music as she sipped her wine and slowly stirred the toasting rice in the pan. It smelled amazing already, she must be hungry.

The hairs on her arm rose just as she felt a presence behind her. Then Joan felt cold hands on her face, covering her eyes. She twisted and flung the wooden spatula she was holding high, splattering some gooey rice on the counter.

"Sorry, sorry! It's just me," Monica nearly shouted, backing away from Joan.

"Holy shit you scared me. Sorry," she said, catching her breath. She felt her heart beating hard in her chest. The moment stretched out where Monica seemed afraid Joan was angry while Joan waited for her body to shift out of fight or flight mode. A deep, breathy laugh escaped her. Monica smiled with her whole face.

"I really am so sorry. I was trying to be cute. Guess I fucked that up," Monica giggled.

"How did you learn to be so quiet? I didn't hear you come in at all."

"I've been living with a podcaster for a few years now. I've learned not to stomp around like I apparently used to," she teased. Joan just rolled her eyes at her.

"Well if I ever need to break in somewhere I'm recruiting you."

"You should. I'd be an excellent thief, I think."

"I think you would too," Joan agreed with a smile and kissed her lightly.

"What are you making me?" Monica asked, eyeing the wooden spatula still in Joan's hand.

"Risotto. And shrimp. Although I haven't started the shrimp. You're home a little earlier than I thought."

"Lucky you. Right?" she teased again. Monica grabbed herself a wine glass as well and poured from the chardonnay open on the counter.

"We may need to open more wine," Joan consulted her computer, checking the recipe, "there is a shocking amount of wine in risotto apparently."

"I think we have another bottle. I'll put it in the refrigerator. Do you want me to make the shrimp? I can." Monica asked.

"No, I got it. You go take a shower or just chill. Dinner will be ready in 20 minutes or so."

Monica didn't have to be told twice. She gave Joan another kiss and took her glass of wine off to the bedroom. Joan heard the shower start a few minutes later. She had started the shrimp when she saw a message pop across her phone's screen.

> I'm going to an influencer event in Houston next weekend. I thought I'd mention in case you were in town, you could attend with me. (This is Carmen!)

Joan smiled at the 'this is Carmen.' She had saved Carmen's number but it's funny to think if she hadn't what she would make of this message. She wiped her hands on the kitchen towel and typed out a message back.

> I'm not planning to be in Houston then, but appreciate the invite. Let's catch up sometime after you are back?

Carmen's reply came back in less than a second.

> For sure!

Joan smiled.

"Who's that? Should I be jealous?" Monica teased, a towel wrapped around her hair. She had on a navy-blue silk robe that had no business being as sexy as it was.

"You? Never. It's Carmen, she's the fashion influencer I met with a couple weeks ago. I had asked if I could go to an event with her, and she's inviting me to one. This one won't work, but she at least remembered me. I honestly couldn't tell how seriously she took my request."

Monica just sighed, "You still don't get how much people like your show, do you?"

"It's just a podcast."

Monica rolled her eyes.

They decided to sit on their back porch to eat dinner. The evening was crisp and perfect. They had almost no yard to speak of but compared to New York it felt like a park. They even had a lemon tree, although neither knew if they were edible. Yes? Probably?

Even with wet hair and her bare feet kicked up on the outdoor coffee table, Monica was a total babe. Joan had felt this way about her since they had first met at a random friend's dinner party three years before. This was the first night that felt normal, like life again. Joan was relieved. Monica seemed content, even joyful. The two laughed as they ate quickly and drank slowly, the sun setting as they did. Eventually it became too brisk and they headed back inside, cuddling on the couch.

"I've been thinking," Monica started, going a little shy for the first time all night. Joan just waited, listened. "Now that we're here, still settling in, but here. I guess, well. I'm not really sure how to say this. I'd like to be a mom one day, and I think I'd really like to be a mom with you." She looked to Joan expectantly. They'd never really discussed children before.

"Oh, wow. That's, well," Joan felt it, this was a moment and she had no idea how to navigate it. "First, I think you'd be an amazing mom. Just amazing. And, I haven't thought that much about it for myself yet."

Silence hung between them. This time it was Joan waiting to see how Monica would react.

"It's a lot to think about. For sure. I guess I just wanted to express that I do want a child someday, and maybe someday soon. We've never talked about it, and it feels important you know."

"OK. Then I'm glad you told me." Joan knew it was the wrong thing to say as soon as it had left her mouth. She could see Monica's face fall a little. "I'm sorry. I'm just, I'm not shocked I just wasn't expecting this tonight."

"No, it's OK. I get it. It's a big conversation," Monica said, "But could I make a suggestion?" A small smile crossed her face, she took another sip of her almost gone wine.

"Yes, please?" Joan awkwardly laughed.

"I'm not looking for you to agree to anything tonight. And we have to be on the same page before anything gets decided," she paused, letting this sink in. "So, for now, why don't you pretend this is one of your interviews. Just be curious about why I want a child, how I might envision them fitting into our lives."

Joan felt a small trickle of guilt hit her. Her partner was making an excellent suggestion, and clearly trying to word it well. And Joan should be curious about this, just like she would be curious for work. She loved learning why people thought things, wanted things, did things. Why not this? Being curious didn't mean she was saying yes, it was just exploring with the woman she loved; getting to know her on another level.

"You're right. I would love to interview you. Shall we begin?" she asked with mock professionalism. Monica just smiled. "Tell me, when did you first think about having a child?"

Monica laid back on the couch more, into Joan's arm, considering. "This is going to sound heavy, I know, but it's the truth. It was when I met you. Growing up, realizing I was gay, I assumed kids just might not be in my future. I didn't know any gay couples, at all, let alone any that had children. So, I really didn't think about it much. But when we started dating, and especially after we moved in together, I don't know. I just started thinking more about the future, like the far future not just next month. And I started picturing a child at some point. Being sleepy newborn parents together. Getting them ready for school together. Lying to them about there being a Santa Claus."

Joan laughed even as she said, "You remember I'm Jewish, right?"

"Santa transcends," Monica said, a wicked smile in her eyes.

"God, I wish I was recording this interview now!" Joan laughed. "OK, next question. If you were to have a child with your partner. How do you see that coming about, adoption? IVF? Steal a cute kid off the street?"

"I would never admit to wanting to steal a child in an interview. Nice try," Monica joked. She settled and thought for a minute. "Honestly, I'd like to try to get pregnant. It looks, I don't know, kind of special. It could be my egg, it could be your egg, I don't feel strongly one way or another on that part."

Joan listened and felt happy they were having this conversation, even though it terrified her on a lot of levels. She couldn't help but think about her conversation with Carmen about pregnancy announcements on social media. What a strange world to be living in. In some ways marvelous, like the fact she and her partner could even be discussing their multiple options to try to have a child; and then on the other hand this world existed that felt angry and hurt. And then Joan started to think about what it would be like to walk around together, the three of them. Here in Los Angeles, probably not many heads would turn at two women with a stroller. But in other parts of the country, like her hometown in southern Missouri, it would not go unnoticed. And although Joan had long ago accepted and even felt pride in this part of herself, she also didn't really like having it on display for the world. It was her business to share or not, and she preferred it that way. She could only imagine all the forms they might have to fill out with a space to fill in the mother's name and then the father's. Would they just write Joan's name in that spot? Her mind started to churn. Monica noticed.

"Can I ask a question now, what are you thinking?"

Joan stopped her spiral. She turned her attention back to the beautiful, smart, sexy, hilarious woman next to her. And she said, "I think I got really lucky in life. And I don't want to fuck that up because of my fears."

Monica gently placed her forehead against Joan's. "You won't. It's OK if you need time to think about all this. It's a lot. Thank you for being curious about my feelings on it." And with that Monica leaned in and kissed Joan deeply, passionately. And then they fucked on the couch.

CHAPTER 10

Pam
@freshlystitched

| **150** POSTS | **32K** FOLLOWERS | **2,593** FOLLOWING |

The nursery Pam worked at was called Shadycreek, although it was nowhere near a creek. It was just west of the downtown area, close enough that on nice days Pam could walk there from her house if she wanted. She didn't often, as she usually had an errand to run before or after work. Or it was just too hot or humid, or way too cold most of the year. But certain times in the late spring and early autumn she would walk. It was a beautiful walk, mostly residential.

As she rounded another corner it occurred to her that she was probably coming up on her two-year anniversary of working at the nursery. She remembered how she walked to work the whole first week, as it was new and exciting, and she couldn't believe her luck to get to work with plants AND be able to walk to work. It was a small miracle really. Although after that first week she hadn't walked for quite some time, no one blamed her. It had been traumatic. She walked past the little blue house, wondering if the family still lived there or if they had moved after the accident. The house didn't look any different, so it was hard to tell.

Pam remembered the way the cool, crisp air had felt in her still slightly damp hair that morning as he walked to her job. She had seen the little boy, backpack slung around his little shoulders exit the house with his mom. He seemed eager, nearly bouncing up and down excited to get on the school bus. His mom called some direction to him as she dashed back into the house. Apparently, they were missing something (the boy's lunch box? a homework assignment?). In the few seconds the boy's mom had ducked back inside, the bus had pulled up to the curb by their house. Pam remembers seeing the little boy, all smiles and excitement, run toward the bus. Clearly, he didn't want to miss it. She heard the mom call his name from the house, only a few paces behind. It happened so quickly it almost hadn't registered for Pam at first. She had been walking toward the bus, on the sidewalk of the other side of the street. She saw the little boy cross the street to reach to the open door of the bus, on the other side, just as another car coming from the opposite direction had sped forward. The driver had not seen the little boy and had ignored the swinging stop sign of the bus. Pam knew the little boy was dead immediately.

She had completely frozen as she watched the rest of the scene play out. The mother, realizing what had happened, ran to her son and cradled his little body in hers. Her clothes had become soaked through with blood within minutes. The bus driver had come around to help the mother, not that there was much he could do. Pam remembered seeing all the little faces pressed up against the bus windows. She remembers seeing the driver of the car standing beside their open car door, seeing the little boy and probably realizing what they had done. It was a young girl, she couldn't have been much older than sixteen. What Pam still doesn't remember is calling 911. But she did, there are records. Or at least she assumes.

She couldn't stand to stick around once the ambulance arrived. She feared she'd have to give a statement to the police or something, so she had walked off to work. She still doesn't feel guilty about this, but she wonders if she should or ever will. She just couldn't stand to be there any longer, there was too much pain. The little boy should have had a longer life, there was so much he didn't experience before he was killed. The young girl, well, Pam doubted she would ever forget that day. She had to live with that mistake forever. The kids on the bus who witnessed such a tragic event, plus who knows, maybe that little boy had a best friend on the bus who saw it all too. And then the mother, that was really what drove Pam to keep walking that day. She couldn't face the mother's pain any longer. It was deafening. It was like seeing a black hole. She knew it would have been better for the mother if the child had never been born, compared to the pain of losing him so tragically. She wondered if the mother blamed herself, wondered what would have happened if she'd just left the packed lunch or whatever had been forgotten in the house. There were so many what ifs that could be chased or imagined.

When she had arrived at work that morning she hadn't told anyone, she just started working. But by lunch the news had spread, and the truth had come out. Her boss had told her she should go home early if she needed to. Pam didn't. What was there to do at her house but think about it? Replay the way the mother had looked when she'd realized what had happened. She stayed for her whole shift, she had even lingered after until she had to go home.

It had taken her a whole year before she had walked to work again, and a year and a half before she took the route that led her by the little blue house. It really was such a lovely walk, she thought to herself and then immediately felt guilty.

When she arrived, she quickly stowed her lunch away in the breakroom refrigerator. Once a quarter they all had a meeting together, before they opened to the public. In many ways it was the most business-like moment of the job as most of the time it felt more like gardening and occasionally ringing customers up. She took a seat, being one of the last to do so. It was a pretty small team, only ten of them. She noticed the new guy on the other side of the room, she still hadn't met him, but it had been less than a week since he started. She realized she was staring when he turned his head and looked back at her. He smiled. Pam quickly looked away, at her feet. Very smooth.

"A couple of quick announcements before we get started," her boss began. Al was in his early sixties and looked every bit a man who'd spent most of his life outside sans sunscreen. He always wore overalls and a baseball cap, even though he was the owner of one of the largest greenhouse and nursery in central Missouri. Al and his wife had hosted a company picnic once, and Pam had noticed they had a shockingly nice house. It was huge. One of those mini mansion type houses in a gated community attached to a country club. She had been surprised at the time.

"First off, we have a new employee. Go ahead and stand up Caleb. I don't always get to embarrass the new ones but your first week fell on a meeting week. Lucky you,' Al joked. Caleb reluctantly stood and gave the group a tentative wave. It was adorable and awkward all at the same time. He didn't look like the typical tan, landscaper type, more like a computer nerd than the kind of guy who would load a fiddle leaf into your hatchback. Pam tried not to stare more. (She failed.)

"Alright. Don't give Caleb too hard a time," Al chuckled as he continued on. "And the second announcement is we will be having our Gold Coin tree removed from the main greenhouse next week. We may need to shut down that area for a half a day or so in order to properly remove it without damaging anything around it. I'll keep you posted." And with that Al went into the usual Profit & Loss updates and customer review notes he did every meeting. But Pam didn't hear any of it. She couldn't believe they were going to remove the Gold Coin (Laburnum Anagyroides). Sure, it didn't make sense why they had one and it didn't bring in any business, but it was so special and so rare. She loved the tree.

The meeting concluded, and everyone started filing out. The scrape of metal chairs on the floor permeated the air as everyone put the break room back together. Pam approached Al before he ducked into his office.

"Before the Gold Coin is removed could I have a cutting?" she asked.

Al gave her a serious face, considering. "Well, I suppose I'd have to take it out of your pay." Pam didn't know what to say to this and was about to open her mouth to agree when Al started laughing.

"I'm kidding! Of course, you can take a cutting. Take two. If I were you I'd probably collect all the seeds I could before they remove it too. I know it's such a waste, but the root system is overgrowing and choking out everything else in the greenhouse. It's a pragmatic decision, but as this place is filled with plant lovers I figured it wouldn't be popular. Anyway, have at it." And with that Al turned and headed to his office, coffee in hand. What Pam didn't tell him was she'd taken seeds before, many times actually. So, it was kind of a relief to finally have official approval.

Her shift passed without much to note, except the new guy, Caleb. She could have sworn she saw him looking her way a few times when they were in the same space. Likely not though, she said to herself. Or if he was, it was probably just to get a sense of his coworkers generally. But still, it didn't feel that way. It felt like interest.

The late afternoon sun was already starting to set, leaving the greenhouse a golden yolky color. Pam carried a burlap bag and shears with her as she approached the Gold Coin. She almost hated to cut a branch off, it felt so different from taking seeds. Seeds fell off on their own, after all. They were only a part of the plant for a time, a whole separate thing. She lovingly touched the shiny green leaves that hung low enough in her reach, choosing her branch.

"Is this your favorite plant here?" a voice behind her asked tentatively. Pam turned and saw Caleb, the owner of the voice. She realized she actually hadn't heard him talk yet, and his voice was much deeper than she would have guessed. She also realized it probably seemed a little odd that she was basically caressing the tree. Great. Normal.

"I've never thought to pick a favorite. But, maybe? She's a really special tree."

"I had to look it up over my break, I had actually never heard of a Gold Coin before."

"And?" Pam asked. Testing him. Seeing what he'd noted about it.

"It's unusual that it's living here, in the Midwest. But this is a greenhouse, full of careful plant-loving weirdos so maybe it's not so strange," he smiled, and Pam got the sense that he included himself in this category. "Also, the seeds are super poisonous. Did you know that?"

"Yes. I did. I googled this plant too. Years ago," Pam said, turning back to the tree. Pulling off a seed and handing it to him. She saw a tiny hesitation in him, before he reached out and took the seed from her, touching her outstretched hand for just a second as he did. Maybe she imagined it, but she thought she saw just a hint of a blush across his pale cheekbones.

"One other fact about Gold Coin trees you won't need the internet to uncover is this," Pam said as she extended her hand toward one of the flowering branches. "The flowers are beautiful. They are my favorite flowers."

"Probably makes it hard for anyone to buy you flowers. Since, this is so rare."

"No one buys me flowers," Pam immediately said with a laugh. But then worried this made her seem as pathetic as she felt. Caleb just smiled back at her.

He turned his gaze toward the blossom she was holding, considering it. The dark crimson petals seemed to unfurl just a little more under his gaze, showing off. And for the first time in a long time Pam felt herself unfurl a little too.

CHAPTER 11

Abby
@alwaysabby

| **5,092** POSTS | **477K** FOLLOWERS | **1,349** FOLLOWING |

Abby had never enjoyed school drop off. It was always such a rushed, chaotic event. Like dropping off someone at the airport; there was the worry you were late and the crush of other cars as you tried to navigate to where you needed to be. Back when their son had been in daycare, and not the giant second grader he was now, her husband had been the drop off parent. But once she had decided to go full time with her influencer career, it had made more sense, or so she had assumed at first, for her to become both the drop off and pick up parent since her schedule was now flexible in a way her husband's was not. If she were being honest, she had grossly underestimated the number of hours she needed in her workday. It turned out flexibility was in some ways just as much of a trap as office hours.

"Davy, don't forget your lunch," she called before her son exited the car without his neon green lunch bag. She had carefully packed it with a thoughtful lunch, something he would eat but not too much junk: almond butter sandwich with fresh strawberries, hummus and carrot sticks, and a no-bake oatmeal cookie. It probably wasn't enough protein but who knew, the nutrition standards seemed to constantly change. She was happy if the food was at least half gone when she opened the bag at the end of the day to clean it before her own personal *Groundhog Day* began again tomorrow.

Abby watched as Davy entered the school, his little feet carrying him across the small campus. She remembered when he was a newborn and could barely roll around on his play mat. It was true what everyone said: the days were long, but the years were short. And it was hard to know if it was the overwhelming love she felt for him, or the sleep deprivation of the last seven years. She had thought it was just the first year that carried so many nights awake, with feedings or fussiness, doing whatever your newborn needed. But she had not been prepared for years after when Davy would go through phases of nightmares or separation anxiety and it felt like every other night she'd wake up to his sweet, sweaty frame on top of hers. It was both the thing she loved most, when he slept on her, and the most annoying thing when what she really needed was a good night's rest or maybe some pleasant morning sex with her husband. Neither was in the cards when Davy invaded their bedroom. But she knew one day she'd be an old lady in her 70s or 80s and just dying to go back to the times when she'd wake up with his ketchup breath in her face, the tiny scowl he always wore in his sleep between his eyebrows, a miniature of his father. For Abby motherhood had been the constant dichotomy between craving her own freedom and personhood while also fiercely wanting to be someone's mother, protector, and at times almost an extension of their body. She wanted to be separate but never apart; it made no sense and yet it was the only thing she'd ever really felt completely certain of.

Twenty minutes later she was pulling into a Joann's parking lot. She loved craft stores; they felt full of possibility. Although today she was just picking up a few styling things for a shoot she needed to do this afternoon. She crossed her fingers they already had some autumn or maybe Halloween things on the shelves, even though it was mid-July. It turned out she was in luck.

"Abby?" She heard a voice behind her as she was picking out some dried flowers. It could be a fan, it could be someone from school, or it could be someone from her past. She wasn't sure which she would prefer at this moment, but she plastered a small smile on her face before turning.

"Yes?"

"Hi, um. This is so random. I feel like I know you," the woman started. Abby had heard versions of this opening line many times before. She wasn't a rock star or anything, but she would sometimes get spotted in places that her demographic would naturally be, or large events like concerts or the airport. It usually happened on days she hadn't had time to put makeup on before rushing off to take her son to school, and today was no exception.

"Hi. I'm Abby. What's your name?" she asked as she extended her hand.

"I'm Reese. I've followed your blog for years. Sorry for bothering you, I just kind of can't believe it's you, like in person."

"Hi Reese. I'm glad you said hi. I really like meeting readers, it's so much better than just saying hi on the internet, you know?" And although Abby had said this exact line many times before, she always meant it.

"Are you working on a blog post right now?" Reese asked with glee.

"Sort of. I'm shooting something for a sponsor this afternoon. I'm really excited about it," and she was; she loved working on seasons ahead. It was weird, but it always made Abby feel like she was getting a little preview into her favorite times of year.

"Ah. That's… well, I usually don't like your sponsored posts as much as the real ones."

"Oh? Sure, I know what you mean," and although Abby did, she also had lots she wanted to add. On the one hand, sure she understood. When she was watching a favorite show and a commercial interrupted it was annoying. But, it also meant she wasn't a subscriber or hadn't paid for the content in any way and how would they keep making great TV if they didn't make money at it somehow? It all made sense. But it always made her feel kind of small when a commenter, or in this case a real-life-in-person reader, said something along these lines.

"Well, thank you for all your support. And I'm really glad you took the time to say hi," Abby said, and she meant it, as she truly was grateful for everything she had. She believed you could work hard, have talent, and at the end of the day you still needed a little bit of luck and support to make it. Whatever your definition of 'make it' was. And she was grateful for it all and not too proud to admit she'd been one of the hard-working AND lucky ones.

She slid into the driver's seat and checked her reflection in the pull-down mirror. She was also grateful Reese hadn't asked for a photo because she could not refuse without seeming rude, but she looked like absolute shit this morning and didn't really want this look frozen forever in timeless halls of the internet. Her red hair looked frizzy and her face was puffy. She knew it was probably shallow to think these kinds of things but there it was. It was nice to feel pretty and today she did not. She checked the clock and saw she'd likely make it home with enough time to throw on a bit of makeup before her RTLAS call. Although those women were her real friends and she'd do the call naked if she had to. But it was nice to have time to put yourself together, to feel like a person. Or at least that's something Abby enjoyed, a little time to listen to a podcast and primp. Maybe if she hurried she'd have enough time to flat iron her hair instead of throwing it up in a claw clip. Again.

She made good use of her time and decided to film herself putting on her makeup. She could edit it into some kind of "get ready with me" video later. If she had time she could even find affiliate links to all her products (or at least the ones she knows her audience will ask about) although she doubted she'd have time. She could always put it up and see what people ask about the most, and just answer those with links. Since she decided to film her makeup routine it took a little longer since she had to set up her camera a few different ways. No time for flat ironing her hair after all. Oh well. A claw clip and some earrings would have to do. She sat down at her computer just a few minutes before the call was supposed to start.

She logged into the call as soon as she saw the first person, Rosie, join. Rosie's cheery, happy face filled Abby's screen.

"Hi! You probably hear this too often already, but you are glowing girl. You just look happy."

Rosie blushed deeper at the compliment. She smiled wide as Leena popped into the chat, followed closely by Carmen.

"Hello, hello. How are you all this fine day?" Carmen nearly chirped from her video window, which was clearly outside as she was walking down a street. She sometimes takes the RTLAS call on a walk, and Abby at first found this annoying until it dawned on her that she was just jealous. She keeps forgetting to take the call on a walk too, why not?

The women began chiming in with their updates, business reports, and laments. For all of them work was picking up as it always does toward the second half of the year when large companies realize they have marketing budget they need to burn before their fiscal year ends and sometimes they turn to influencers. Carmen and Leena solidified their plans, as Carmen would be in Houston for an event and the two would be meeting with Carmen staying in Leena's guest bedroom. Abby wished she had a trip coming up, sounded nice to get away. Although if something did pop up she'd probably decline, not wanting to miss any of the holiday season with her son, which reminded her:

"Rosie, you haven't really updated us on pregnancy stuff. Obviously, your skin looks dewy and your boobs look amazing but other than that how are things?" Abby asked.

"Oh, good. It's overall good," she said with a sigh.

"Are strangers already giving you the mom guilt? Ignore, ignore, ignore. Even an old spinster like me knows how shaming the internet can be to moms. It's just stupid," Carmen guessed.

"Well, yes, but it's not that. Actually, a good friend of mine, Jackie. She's a doctor. I think I've mentioned her to you all before. Anyway, she was pregnant too, basically the same timeline as me. And I just heard from her a couple days ago that she had a miscarriage. I think it was bad, she was in the hospital for a day or two."

"Oh, I'm so sorry Rosie," Abby said. Rosie just nodded, the other women could see the tears forming at the edges of her eyes.

"And, well, I swear I'm not trying to make that about me. But I just keep thinking if it happened to her, with all her medical knowledge and just knowing how strong she is, then maybe I'm next. I know that's kind of ridiculous, but I just can't get it out of my head," and with this admission Rosie started to cry. The women gave her a few moments, not wanting to overwhelm.

"Well, have you been to your doctor recently?" Carmen asked cautiously.

"Yes."

"And, everything was OK? They didn't have any concerns or things you needed to change like your diet or something?"

"No. Everything was fine. And maybe it will be. It just seemed so sudden for Jackie. It makes no sense and it makes the whole thing feel so random and fragile," Rosie said.

"We're so sorry for your friend. That's really hard," Abby said. And then the call was silent for a little bit, no one really knowing what else to say.

"This is the worst possible segue I'm sure, but I have some news," Leena started, although she was speaking so softly Carmen had to ask her to move closer to the microphone on her laptop, which she did.

"I'm, well, I'm also pregnant," Leena confessed. The women's eyes went wide, and the mood instantly changed. There were shouts and giggles and congratulations all around.

"I'm only 14 weeks, but I figure I might as well tell you since I feel like Carmen will find out when she visits next week anyway. My husband will not stop talking about it, he's so excited," Leena explained and then quickly added, "I'm excited too."

Abby noted the hesitation in Leena's voice, but she decided not to press it. She could tell from her face that Carmen felt the same way. Parts of motherhood and being a woman in the world generally were just a lot, and you didn't need to explain it all since there were probably times you couldn't anyway. If Leena had more to share with the group she would, in her own time. Or at least Abby hoped so.

"Well, shit. I'm sorry for bringing up my friend who lost her baby," Rosie said, wiping her tears off her cheeks. "I'm so happy for you!"

"Rosie, don't worry about it. You're fine! I'm fine. And I'm really sorry for your friend," Leena reassured. Rosie knew Leena wasn't the type to be superstitious, but she couldn't help but feel the fact she had brought up miscarriage just as Leena was announcing her pregnancy was a bad omen. Like, she had somehow cursed Leena. If she were being honest, she sort of felt she had cursed Jackie too as her miscarriage happened the same day they had met for lunch. But no, that was ridiculous, she told herself as she reminded her body to breathe.

CHAPTER 12

Pam
@freshlystitched

| **152** POSTS | **32K** FOLLOWERS | **2,596** FOLLOWING |

P am watered a bed of bunny ear cactus (Opuntia Microdasys) inside the main green house. For a proud plant-lady she'd never really liked cacti. For one, it didn't make much sense to grow and maintain them in the Midwest. Although she did like lots of other tropical plants that didn't belong anywhere near Missouri. If she were honest she knew it was because they were so popular. It was annoying how many women she followed online had cacti in their house, in the background of their photos or videos. It felt like a styling prop. And this was probably why they had a giant bed of bunny ear cactus at her work, they were great sellers.

She saw Caleb emerge from the breakroom. It appeared he was getting off, he must have had the early shift today. He caught her eye. Clearly he'd noticed she was looking at him, so she gave him a nod as if to say 'hi, bye, I acknowledge your presence' and then turned back to her work. To her surprise, he started to walk over toward her. When she was sure he was actually walking in her direction she stopped misting the plants around her, so the little cloud of water could dissipate before she misted Caleb too.

"Hey, um, look, historically I've been no good at this so I'm just going to say it. Could I take you out sometime? Actually, maybe tonight. Could I take you out tonight?"

Pam felt shocked. She hadn't allowed herself to really believe he'd be interested in her, even though they clearly had flirted a few times. Sometimes men did that, probably out of boredom or because they were insecure and needed women around them to want them. She'd also rarely had a man be this straightforward with her. Usually a first date was lightly veiled by some other reason they were hanging out, she supposed, so if they guy changed his mind he could pretend it hadn't been a date in the first place. She also realized she was taking too long to answer and it was probably going to hurt his feelings if she didn't say something soon.

"Yes. I'd like that. Tonight is great," she said. And then immediately worried if saying she was free tonight made her look like a loser. Like she didn't have anything going on (which she didn't). Maybe he'd think she never had anything going on (which was mostly true).

"Great. What time works for you? Maybe seven?"

"Seven is good. It's great," she added and then felt mortified. This whole exchange was just shocking to her. Who did this? What was this?

"OK. I'll be honest, I hadn't thought of where or any kind of plan. I'll text you?" he asked. She wondered if he had been worried she'd say no. Had anyone ever said no to him before? He was so cute. And then they did the awkward business of exchanging numbers, so he could actually text her later. Pam felt both thrilled and a little anxious to see his name in her contacts list.

The rest of her shift seemed to float by in a pleasant mist. She was going on a date, with Caleb. Who was she? She hadn't been on a date in so long, did she even know how to interact with the opposite sex anymore? Shortly after her divorce she'd tried online dating, but it had been a disaster. She hated creating a profile in the apps and checking them, and all the little mind games it turned into for her. Plus, her town was just small enough that it was awkward seeing the profile of people you knew on there. The whole thing had just been weird. The few dates she had been on had also been weird, and mostly short. Nothing had materialized from that awful social experiment and so she'd basically given up on the whole idea since then.

It didn't help that her ex had basically started dating immediately after their divorce; someone from work and she suspected it had started before they were actually broken up. In fact, looking back she kind of thought this other woman might have been partially the reason they had split. She tried not to think about it, but it nagged at her when it came up in her mind. Wasn't that kind of the most unsupportive, unfeminist thing you could do? Destroy another woman's family, especially if it was clear she was going through a hard time? The girl was nearly ten years younger than Pam, so in some ways she didn't blame her—certainly not as much as she blamed her ex. It was all just so cliché.

She pushed these thoughts out and focused on the fact that she had a date tonight. She felt nervous. She had worked her way around the greenhouse, tending to the tasks she had that day. She loved growing things, seeing them blossom and thrive. It was proof she actually mattered, actually existed.

The spot where the Gold Coin tree had been was still just a big patch of dirt. The stump had been ground and some of the upper root system had been dug up too. She assumed the plan was to fill the space in with more dirt and at least for a time plant something with a shallow root system or that only needed a short time in the earth before being moved to pots and sold. But she hadn't really heard. She missed the tree. As silly as she knew it was, it felt like a friend had moved away. Her cutting was still alive at home, but the little roots it sprouted so far didn't seem substantial enough to plant. She was unsure if she would plant it ever, as she didn't have a large greenhouse like this, so it probably wouldn't survive the winters outside if she did. She had gathered a lot of seeds before they removed the tree, but she was already running low on those too. Things were coming to a natural end, she thought. Maybe it meant something new would start, and she thought of her date that night but tried not to hope too much.

After her shift she walked home. She was keeping up the walking habit for now. But this left her a slightly sweaty mess, so she took a quick shower and rushed to dry her hair. Caleb had texted that he would pick her up, who did that? And had asked for her address. She had just finished getting ready and it was 6:58. For one second, she considered taking a shot of rum; she was nervous. But she didn't want him to smell it on her breath. Plus, why get all worked up over this guy, right? She didn't even know him that well yet. She heard a knock at her door at 7:01. He was on time. She looked around and realized she hadn't made time to pick up, not that it mattered. She answered the door and immediately stepped outside. Caleb was wearing black pants and denim shirt, not all that different from their work clothes but certainly cleaner. He smelled like the woods, but in a very cologne-from-a-store kind of way. It was nice.

"Hi."

"Hi."

"You look really nice," Caleb said.

"You smell nice," she blurted. Then immediately sucked in her breath, with regret. He noticed. "Sorry. That was so cheesy. It just came out," she said. He smiled.

"Probably a little different from my usual scent, dirt," he joked. And Pam giggled. She couldn't believe she giggled. What the fuck was wrong with her?

"So, and you can say no, but I saw that there was a Thai place just a few blocks from here. Would you want to walk there to get dinner? Or is that a place you go a lot, since you live here, and maybe that's too boring?"

"No, that sounds good. I love Thai."

Caleb started to head in the opposite direction of the restaurant. OK, so he's directionally challenged. Good, not perfect. She was starting to get worried.

"Actually, it's this way," she said as she started to lead the way. Caleb followed.

Dinner was really nice, if not a little awkward at first. They mostly talked about plants and how they got into working at the greenhouse. They had both ordered a glass of wine with their meal, but it just wasn't the kind of place where you ordered multiple drinks, so Pam still felt mostly nervous and anxious the entire time. Maybe she should have had a shot of rum before, to take the edge off. At the end of the meal they split the check. Caleb tipped in cash and she tried not to look but she saw he was a good tipper. Another good sign. He reached the door first as they left and held it open for her. She kept waiting for him to be an asshole but so far there really wasn't anything, which made her even more anxious.

They walked back toward her house and his car, the evening air was that perfect temperature that's absolutely impossible to get indoors.

"Tell me something about you that I don't know," Caleb said.

"What?"

"I know you love plants and Thai food. Same same. But tell me something that I don't know yet."

"Hmm. OK, but then you have to tell me something too," she challenged.

"Deal."

Pam thought for a moment and decided since it all felt too good to be true maybe she should push a little, see what the universe really had going on. Was that instinct the self-sabotaging part of herself or the honest part?

"I'm divorced. I was married for almost four years. We divorced a couple years ago. It was messy." That was all she offered up at first; she waited to see how that spoonful would go down for him. They kept walking and for a few beats Caleb didn't say anything. Probably he was reformulating his idea of her in his mind, now that he knew she was damaged goods and undesirable. Obviously there had to be something wrong with her, otherwise her husband wouldn't have left.

"Are you going to say anything?" she asked.

"I'm sorry. That sounds painful. Also, I'll be honest, you seem too young to have already been married and divorced. I'm kind of surprised I guess."

"We got married pretty young. I thought it was really romantic at the time."

Caleb just nodded.

"Sorry, but can you tell me what you're thinking? Because I'm starting this whole story in my head now where you think a lot less of me," Pam said.

"Oh no! I don't think less of you. Actually, I was thinking about my mom. So, here's one thing you don't know about me. My parents divorced when I was really little, I guess I would have been one or maybe two. I don't remember it. I never really knew my dad. So my mom is divorced, and I certainly don't think poorly of her. I love my mom, she's the best."

"Got it. OK, good. I mean, not good that your parents are divorced and you didn't know your dad. Just, that you don't think less of me," Pam stammered.

"Yeah. Like I said, I don't really remember him or life with him around. My mom does, obviously, so I think it was a lot worse for her."

They had reached the front of her house. Her small porch had string lights lining the outside and she'd turned them on before they left. Now they looked so quaint and she was glad she had.

"Do you want to come in? I have wine, and rum, or I could make coffee or something." Pam wasn't ready for the night to end. Plus, it felt weird to leave things on this kind of sad note they had stumbled on together.

"Sure. I'll take a glass of wine."

They climbed the few stairs of her porch and she unlocked her front door. As Pam turned the light switch on she immediately remembered she hadn't picked up before she left. Her house wasn't a pigsty by any means, but this was not exactly the impression she had wanted to give. She quickly led him through to the kitchen, where she grabbed two glasses and opened a bottle of Zin. Caleb looked around her kitchen as she did. She hadn't realized before how big her collection of wine bottles and spirits was getting. It looked like a pretty impressive bar, better than some restaurants. It wasn't until someone new was in your space that you saw things through their eyes, and fresh judgements emerged.

"I like your mug collection," he said. She had an open shelf above her coffee maker with all handmade mugs. She'd started collecting them a few years ago and it had grown fast. She really didn't need more than ten mugs for just her, but they were all unique and special. She loved collecting them from handmade artists she followed online. She wanted to make a few of her own eventually, but she didn't have a wheel or a kiln so she planned to take a pottery class. She just hadn't made time yet.

"Thanks. I have too many, but I love them." She handed Caleb a glass of wine and led him toward her sunroom. They had to walk past her studio to get to the sunroom and the door was open wide, which she never would have left open if she'd thought she was going to have company. Panic gripped her as she saw Caleb's head turn and look inside for one brief moment as she ushered him forward. She could tell he had seen it.

"Hey, um, was that a crib?"

Pam let out a deep sigh. "Yes. Sorry, I would have shut the door. I wasn't planning to invite you in. Now this feels like a scene in a sitcom where two characters go on a first date and then the guy finds the girl wearing a wedding dress the next day and she's all 'wait, I can explain.'"

Caleb smiled at her joke, but then clearly was waiting for her to explain.

"No, I don't have a kid. I don't even want kids. I sew things. Like, I have a shop on Etsy and make lots of different things but one that has been very popular for me is baby quilts. And I photograph them on the crib in there. It's good marketing. I also have a bunch of dress forms and I use those life-size plastic skeletons to photograph clothes I make like patchwork jackets," She had never had to explain this out loud to someone before. And although everything she was saying was technically true, it felt like the biggest cover up story ever.

Caleb seemed to relax. He pulled out his phone.

"What's your Etsy shop? I want to see your work. You should have made that your thing I didn't know. Not that you shouldn't have said you're divorced, that really lightened the mood for the night," he joked.

"Hey! You're the one who doesn't have a dad," she joked back, then immediately regretted it.

"Whoa, too soon. Too soon," he said. But she could tell he was teasing her. She still felt bad.

She took his phone and pulled up Instagram. She typed in her shop's name, and then handed the phone back.

"You can see more of my work on my Instagram account than you can in my shop right now. I need to restock."

Caleb set down his wine and began scrolling. He clicked on various pictures and said how much he liked her work. He seemed genuinely impressed. She saw he clicked the follow button too.

"So, this is the crib?" he asked, pointing to a photo of a baby quilt she had made, draped over the edge of a simple wooden crib.

"Yes, that's it. It's in a lot of my photos actually."

"Do people think you have a baby?" he asked.

"Probably. To be honest I don't think anyone really thinks about my personal life. It's not that kind of account, it's mostly just my work. I rarely post other things. I have before but I usually end up deleting them. I guess I only feel comfortable sharing the projects I'm working on for my shop. That's mostly what I started the account for anyway, for marketing."

It felt weird to talk so sincerely about her work. She hoped it didn't sound like she took herself super seriously or anything. It was just a hobby, another thing to do with her hands beyond caring for plants. But she was proud of it.

"Well, your work is really cool. I didn't know you were internet famous. Isn't 32,000 followers a lot?"

"It's, I don't know, good? Anyway, thanks."

They chatted more, drank the wine she had opened. She gave him a tour of her house plants. She asked if he had house plants and he admitted he did. He said he'd have to show her next time, which felt almost like a second date invitation.

"Well, I probably should be going," Caleb said. It was nearly midnight. They had talked for hours. Pam felt light and airy, sure it was the wine, but it was also him. No one had made her feel this good in a long time. She was certain she didn't deserve it. She led him to the door and prayed she didn't have terrible wine teeth. She opened the door and Caleb had to step around her to get out, so she smelled his cologne again. He must have noticed. As he stood close he looked deeply into her eyes. He didn't say anything, but it felt like a question and he was searching for an answer. She didn't look away or move. Then, slowly, he leaned in and kissed her. She realized she hadn't been kissed in, well, a long time and she didn't know what to do with her hands. But then he was pulling away. He took a step back, outside the front door. He smiled. She smiled back.

CHAPTER 13

Leena
@leenacooks

| **1,989** POSTS | **202K** FOLLOWERS | **653** FOLLOWING |

eena set out the cheeses she had bought to make a fancy cheese board. She had maybe gone a little overboard for the weekend. She knew Carmen would be busy at her event most of the time, but this hadn't stopped her from planning a cheese board and tea snack for this afternoon when she got in, new sheets and fresh flowers in the guest bedroom, and she already had a candle going in the hallway bathroom which would be Carmen's during her stay. Leena rarely had house guests. In fact, since she and her husband moved to Houston seven years ago, they'd only had family visit twice in all that time. It wasn't that they weren't close, they would make the trek to India at least every other year to see both sets of their parents. It was harder for their parents to visit, being such a long flight. And while Leena was an only child, her husband's brother and his family never visited overnight as they only lived about an hour away.

Since the guest bedroom rarely got used, it wasn't a big tragedy that soon it would become the nursery. She already had the furniture and wallpaper picked out. She was just waiting a couple more months before pulling the trigger. She figured she could probably hit Black Friday sales for most of the big items and save some money.

Leena filled small bowls with nuts and dried fruits. She had multiple sets of cheese knives, and she chose a set that was made of wood and even included a tiny ax for the harder cheeses. She artfully smeared hummus and a fruit jam along one edge. She liked putting together a fancy cheese board, it was a joy to have an excuse to do so. Just as she was unwrapping the still cold cheese, she heard the doorbell ring. She had offered to pick up Carmen from the airport, but Carmen had insisted she'd just get an Uber. Leena set out the box of tea bags by the cheeseboard and headed to answer the door.

"Hello, hello, hello!" Carmen squealed as she pulled Leena into a big hug. "God, I am so excited for this weekend. I am so glad this all worked out. And thank you again."

"Me too. I'm so glad you are in town, it's really a treat. I honestly love hosting," Leena said.

Carmen rolled her suitcase just inside the door and ducked back out, did she have more luggage for the weekend? Leena wondered. She emerged again almost immediately with a couple of packages in her arms.

"Mail call. Just kidding. These were on your front porch," she said and handed the packages to Leena.

"Oh, thanks. Probably work stuff."

"I get it. That's what I wish they would tell you. 'Do you want to be an internet person? Well, get ready for endless boxes in your entryway'" Carmen joked. Leena led the way toward the kitchen, and Carmen instinctively followed.

"It's true. I've had legitimate fights with my husband about boxes before. And I don't have half the following you do, I bet it's terrible," Leena said with a laugh.

"Holy shit Leena! Did you put this together just for us? My mouth is literally watering," Carmen said as she eyed the cheeseboard, immediately diving in.

"I thought you could use a snack after your flight. Travel always takes it out of me."

"I'm going to always stay with food bloggers if this is what a little travel snack is to you. Wow."

Leena blushed at the compliment. It was a beautiful board, she had to admit. She started to heat her kettle to make tea. Carmen gushed over the box of tea bag options too, saying it was like a five-star hotel. She picked out a mint and orange tea bag, while Leena opted for passion fruit. She was completely out of ginger tea as she had consumed it almost exclusively her entire first trimester. It was the only thing that didn't make her feel nauseated.

"Well, do you want to do a little unboxing? See what these packages are?" Carmen asked.

"We can. Honestly, it's probably just cans of coconut milk. That campaign I told you guys about is starting soon," Leena reached for her kitchen shears, to cut open the boxes.

"Exciting. I can't wait to see the recipes. And I hope you know I was mostly joking before, about all the boxes. It's actually really fun to get things sometimes. I would just die when a package or letter arrived for me when I was a kid, so if I could have known how much mail I'd get as an adult I would have been thrilled."

"Same. It's mostly just funny. Although I wasn't joking about it being a marital fight. Ha ha."

"I wouldn't know. But I can imagine coming home to a bunch of boxes would be pretty annoying," Carmen said.

"Hey! Whose side are you on?" Leena joked.

Carmen threw her hands up, "Yours. Of course. Fuck your sweet husband," Carmen said with a wink.

Leena had the first box open and it was not coconut milk after all. She pulled a jewel-toned baby quilt from the box. It had intricate stitching along the front and back. It was actually breath-taking it was so beautiful. Leena felt a few tears come to her eyes.

"Wow, that's gorgeous," Carmen commented as she sipped her tea and sliced another wedge of cheese.

"Let me just snap a photo real quick so I don't forget to post about this," Leena said as she quickly took out her phone and took a photo of the card it came with next to the quilt.

"This girl contacted me just after I announced my pregnancy. She makes these quilts and other things and she offered me one. They are so pretty I accepted. Of course, she said no-strings attached but I'll post about it, try to get her more business."

"Every free gift has strings. Not that I'm complaining. But no one just wants to give us something, it's a part of their marketing to get us to post about whatever they send us."

"It's true. Normally I don't accept things. I don't really like giving out my address. But her quilts were so pretty I just couldn't help myself," Leena said with a sheepish smile.

"It's a beautiful quilt. And I'm sure the girl meant well, I'm not trying to say she didn't. It's all good anyway. Why complain about getting a gift, that's just dumb," Carmen said with a sly smile.

Leena sliced open the second box and began to pull out small things. There was a lotion, a candle, some bath bombs, and a shell necklace that wasn't particularly her style. Carmen noticed too, it was a pretty random box.

"Huh. No note. I can't even send a thank you," Leena said looking confused. She checked the box for a return address but there wasn't one. It had been shipped from somewhere in Kansas, not any place she recognized.

"I get random gifts sometimes too. I feel like it's usually from an agency I've worked with or something like that. Someone who already has my address. Although usually there is a card because, again, strings are attached," Carmen said, picking up the candle. "This smells amazing," she held to Leena's nose. She sniffed. It did.

"I don't normally get boxes like that, I think it's different for food bloggers maybe. But ever since announcing my pregnancy I have gotten a lot more messages and things so it's probably a congrats gift I guess."

"Speaking of, I got you something," Carmen said, and she pulled a small package from her oversized handbag. She handed the wrapped gift to Leena.

"Carmen, you didn't have to do that," she said even as she was already pulling off the ribbon and opening it. Inside was a pair of baby moccasins in sage green. They were tiny, and they were adorable.

"Oh! These are so cute. I love them! Thank you," she said, hugging Carmen.

The two devoured the cheeseboard, Leena was proud. She showed Carmen to the guest bedroom and gave her space to change and freshen up before her event that evening. Her husband, Ramesh, wouldn't be home for a few more hours. So he and Carmen likely wouldn't meet until the morning as Leena assumed Carmen would stay out for drinks and networking late. Who knew, maybe she'd meet someone and stay out really late. It was Carmen after all. She was the fun one. And although Leena knew that made her the not-as-fun one, she didn't care. She'd always been a homebody. She'd like to have excuses to stay home, tucked away and quietly enjoying her life. That's probably at least partly why she got into cooking. And now she dreamed of her evenings, and life really, being filled with a tiny baby and then a toddler and then an elementary kid and all the snacks and play and colorful artwork that would eventually clutter their refrigerator door. She could not think of a better life. She was thrilled.

Leena was putting away the washed and dried wooden board when Carmen emerged down the stairs in a stunning leopard print two-piece set. The top was a tasteful crop top and the pants were fitted but cut like fancy slacks. Where did she shop, Leena wondered, she always looked so glamorous.

"I know, I know, it's a bit much. But I love an animal print and I just couldn't resist. Plus, I figure if you're going to show up over-dressed anywhere, a fashion blogger convention might make the most sense ever."

"You look perfect. I could never pull something like that off."

"Don't put yourself down to flatter me. You're gorgeous and you know it," Carmen said.

Leena did not know it, but it was nice to hear. Her pants had just started to feel tight against her growing bump, so she'd take any compliment she could.

"Have fun, and we'll just leave the front door unlocked so stay out as late as you like."

"I always do," Carmen said with a laugh. She kissed Leena lightly on the check before she said goodbye and hopped into her waiting Uber.

Leena looked around her empty, tidy house. She didn't plan to start cooking dinner until Ramesh was home. She was making steaks with garlic butter broccoli for the side and the meal didn't take long to come together. She finished flattening the boxes that had arrived and put them in the recycling bin outside. She put the baby quilt on the edge of an armchair in her bedroom, she was excited to show Ramesh once he was home. She put the rest of the items in her bathroom, lighting the candle as she did. Almost all scents had been completely repugnant to her just last month but now she could enjoy them again. This candle smelled like cinnamon and blueberry, almost like a pie but not sugary sweet like some food candles smelled. It was subtle. She decided to kill some time and take a bath too, why not?

She was just wrapping her lavender colored robe around herself when she heard the front door, her husband was home. She twisted up her hair and padded downstairs in her bare feet. She felt her stomach twist and churn, and she thought she must be hungry again.

Ramesh greeted her at their kitchen island. He was thumbing through the letters, or more likely bills, she left on the counter. He kissed her deeply and for a quick second slipped his hand under her robe and cupped her breast. She knew they'd gotten bigger too, in addition to her waistline. Clearly Ramesh had been noticing as well. She felt him lean in, caressing her body. She stepped back, holding her hand to her stomach.

"What's wrong?" he asked, with concern in his eyes. She knew Ramesh was probably just as excited about their pregnancy as her, maybe more. He'd wanted to start a family almost as soon as they'd been married. It was she who'd wanted to start her career first.

"Nothing. I think I'm just hungry I guess. My stomach feels weird."

"Let's make dinner then. What can I do?"

"Can you start the broiler? I'm making steaks and that broccoli you like," she said, starting to pull things from the refrigerator. The cool air felt good on her face. She didn't feel well but that was something she was getting accustomed to.

"Let me cook. I know how to make it. You should just sit down, put your feet up," he said. Normally she would decline; she liked cooking together. But maybe putting her feet up would help. She pulled the robe closer in around her and laid herself across the couch in the nearby living room. She could still see Ramesh across the kitchen island, so she could still direct the dinner even if she wasn't making it. A heavy headache began to settle into her forehead; maybe she was getting a migraine. She closed her eyes as things began to feel a little swirly around her. She thought she heard Ramesh ask her something, but it sounded far off as if she was under water. She could feel herself drifting.

When Leena awoke she heard the foreign sounds of beeps and clicks. She bolted upright, causing Ramesh to rush to her side.

"It's OK. You're OK. We're at the hospital," he said.

She took in her surroundings and sure enough, it was as he said. She was in a hospital bed, her lavender robe gone and starchy hospital gown in its place. She felt confused and everything felt like the edges were fuzzy.

"What happened?" she asked. Her husband was about to answer just as someone rushed in.

"Leena! Oh my god!" Carmen half yelled as she rushed into the room. She was in the same outfit from earlier that night but now it looked crumpled and had taken on a menacing edge. Carmen looked frantic. Ramesh took her shoulders, in a kind of half hug, half holding her back stance.

"I'm Ramesh. You must be Carmen. Leena's going to be OK," he said to her in a reassuring but firm tone, as if he was unsure of her mental state. "Wait, how did you find us?"

"I got back to your house and no one was there, but there was... blood. There was a lot of blood." Carmen's eyes darted to Leena in the hospital bed. "I called the police, and I called the hospital. They said you were here. So, I came too." Carmen started to cry, something Leena had never seen before. It scared her almost as much as waking up in the hospital had. Carmen just wasn't the type of person who cried easily.

"We left in an ambulance. We're still not sure what happened but Leena said her stomach hurt and she needed to lay down. When I looked back she was passed out and there was blood on the couch. I called 911. Honestly, I totally forgot you were staying with us this weekend. I'm sorry," Ramesh explained. This was the first Leena was hearing this side of the story too.

"Oh, don't apologize. I was just so scared. I thought Leena had been murdered. Thank god you're OK."

A doctor entered the room with a nurse at his side. He assessed Carmen's outfit but made no comment. He turned his attention toward Leena and spoke quietly.

"Leena, glad to see you're awake. How are you feeling?" he said slowly, as if trying not to startle a lost cat.

"Did I lose my baby?" was all she could say. His expression didn't change, but from the look on his nurse's face she knew. She started to scream.

CHAPTER 14

Ela
@justanotherela

| **58** POSTS | **599** FOLLOWERS | **852** FOLLOWING |

She had finally done it. Ela had listed their brand-new-never-been-used-before crib online. Starting back to work had derailed some of her cleaning and organizing goals, but she knew it was time. She needed a fresh start. She deserved a fresh start after everything she'd been through, and the crib had to go. She had expected it would sell fast. Considering it was brand new, she felt like she was almost giving it away for how cheap she'd listed it. But so far, nothing. She tried not to panic, she tried to remain hopeful. It was annoying how little things like this, not being able to sell a crib, could make her completely spiral. She knew exactly where her mind would go if she didn't get a few potential buyers soon. She'd feel stuck again. Stuck in life and stuck with this useless crib she should have made James move. No one would buy it and it would sit in her house, mocking her.

Ela opened her laptop, which was generally what she did when she felt the deep sadness starting to suck at her lungs. Distraction was always good. She had started checking this message board recently and had kind of become a regular commenter, which was so unlike her. She usually preferred to lurk rather than leave comments. It had started when James told her she had a Medea complex. It was during one of their very last fights, as he was moving out. Ela had no idea what he was talking about, but she didn't admit it to him at the time. After he'd left she looked it up.

It turned out Medea was Greek mythology. The character Medea kills her two sons as an act of revenge on her husband who leaves her for another woman. She didn't know if James really thought she had miscarried on purpose because she didn't want to be married to him. Honestly, she had no idea what he meant, but of course he made the miscarriage about him. And it was such a cruel thing to say. While Ela had been searching online to learn what a Medea complex was, she had stumbled upon this message board. There was a whole thread mocking the myth, pointing out how it was so obviously written by a man who needed to be the center of everything, which had made Ela laugh. Some commenters pointed out that maybe Medea didn't want to be a mother anymore. And also, why had the two children been left to Medea to care for after her husband trotted off to shack up with someone new?

The message board was a mixture of dark humor coupled with people being honest about not wanting children or even questioning whether anyone should have kids. She learned Medea was considered one of the first references to neonaticide, which she then had to look up too. And now her search history included things like 'baby hatch' and 'antinatalism.'

Finally she closed her laptop. She had successfully distracted herself. She was getting better and better, see? Ela continued filling boxes with other baby items as well as some things she just didn't want anymore because they reminded her of life with James. These were things like a beautiful marble vase, a wedding gift from his parents. If he didn't want it, she wasn't obligated to keep it around. Into the box it went. She also cleaned out her closet. Her weight had fluctuated so much this past year, it was time to donate the old and buy some new (used) things. She put the boxes in the back of her car and drove across town to her favorite thrift store.

She parked on the side, where donations were accepted. She didn't mind putting the boxes by the door herself as she didn't need a donation receipt. But the day must have been slow because someone came out to help her. She popped her trunk and reach to hand the man the first box.

"Don't worry, I got it," he said as he reached past her to grab things. Ela felt weird just standing there while he unloaded her donations so she picked up one of the trash bags of clothes and carried it over toward the door.

"No really, I can get it all for you. It's no trouble," he insisted.

"OK. Thanks," Ela said.

"How old's your kiddo?" he asked. Ela's stomach dropped. She just stared at him. He gestured at the box that held some of the baby things. "Mine's always growing out of her stuff so fast too," he said with a wink.

"I don't have any kids," she stammered. The man looked confused as he grabbed the last bag in her trunk. Before he could say anything else Ela slammed the trunk door closed and turned to get back in the front seat. She pulled her car around and parked in front of the store. She took a few deep breaths. It was fine. Honest mistake. He was just trying to chat. She pulled out her phone and scrolled while she let her breathing return to normal.

She had intended to go thrifting; that's why she had driven to this specific store. But now, Ela wasn't in the mood. Instead she started her car and drove a few blocks down to a fabric store. She didn't have anything in mind, but she wasn't ready to go home yet. And she could spend her money and time however she wanted. She didn't have to get home to relieve the babysitter. She was free. Maybe it was time to start a new project. She had this idea for repurposing old band shirts into dresses by sewing bandanas or quilted fabrics on the bottom. She was going to make one for herself and if it turned out how she hoped maybe she'd make more. Maybe she'd start selling them or something. A new project sounded like just the thing she needed.

CHAPTER 15

Carmen
@carmenelectric

| **7,224** POSTS | **672** FOLLOWERS | **872** FOLLOWING |

Carmen saw Joan was already sitting by the counter, with a steaming mug in front of her. She checked her phone, no she wasn't late. Joan must've been early. They were meeting in Pasadena this time, for breakfast. Since this was closer to Joan's neighborhood, she supposed it made sense she would beat her here. Carmen caught her eye and waved as she headed in her direction.

"Good to see you," Carmen said as she kissed Joan's cheek lightly. Joan mimicked the gesture.

"You too. Thank you again for inviting me to your event last week, even though it didn't work out. I honestly never know if I will hear from people again after we meet. As you can imagine, sometimes I come off like the exploitative journalist I am," Joan said dead pan. Carmen let out a small cackle.

"Well, I can't get enough attention. As you know. So, I'm looking forward to being exploited," Carmen mustered a small smile. It may have been a heavy week, but she wanted to be in good spirits even if she didn't feel it. She picked up a menu and gave it a once over, pretty typical diner fare. Eggs cooked every which way with variations on sides of meat and potatoes. She loved a greasy spoon, even though she rarely ate at them. She had worked at one briefly, before she realized better tips happened in the evening and then she quickly got a job at a bar instead. That's what she had been doing before she became whatever it was she was now.

Soon their server materialized and took their orders. To Carmen's surprise, Joan ordered French toast and when the server asked if she wanted whipped cream she said yes. Why she found this surprising she'd have to figure out later, but there it was. Carmen had two eggs over easy with hash browns and a coffee. Their young server left, and the two women sat for a moment. Something about it felt like a first date. Carmen could feel she was off her game a little, not feeling her jovial self.

"So, how was the event? I know you said it was for AMT. I had to google it after, and now I understand they are the largest affiliate network in the world. Seems like most influencers, especially those in fashion or home use it," Joan said. Clearly, she had done her homework. It must be fun peering into other people's worlds for a living, getting to escape your own for a time, Carmen thought.

"The event was good. I met up with a few friends, learned about some of the new features and changes AMT is doing this year. Actually, I spoke on a panel. It was kind of a Q&A type thing, not a speech or anything. It was good." Joan could tell Carmen was not her usual self even though they'd only officially met once before. Something was off.

"Is everything OK?" she asked. Carmen sighed.

"Actually, no. I was staying with my friend Leena, she's in my RTLAS group. It stands for Rising Tide Lifts All Ships, you know that saying? She's a food blogger. Our group is just four of us. We're all influencers and we meet once a month to talk shop. Anyway, I was staying at Leena's because she and her husband live in Houston. While I was there she, well she had a miscarriage and it was pretty traumatic. She was in the hospital." Joan's eyes widened. Carmen continued, "She's OK. But yeah, she lost the baby. It was awful. And it was so strange because I saw her before my event, she was fine, she seemed great really. Glowing. And then when I got back to their house no one was home, but there was blood everywhere. I thought maybe someone had broken in, or I didn't know what to think. Eventually I found her and husband at the hospital and she was OK, but they lost the baby."

"I'm so sorry," Joan said and reached across to hold Carmen's hand for a brief moment. Carmen felt the soft squeeze before Joan removed her hand again.

"Me too. Leena is devastated." Their food arrived, the smells of sweet French toast and salty potatoes filling the air between them. Carmen set her napkin in her lap, although now she didn't feel like eating.

"It felt so weird going back to the conference the next day. I almost didn't. I also got a hotel, so they could have their space but that almost felt like a betrayal too. Like I was leaving her when she was in need. Anyway, not to make this story about me. Although clearly, I am," Carmen said with a half-hearted laugh. Being self-deprecating felt like a good way to steer this conversation to something else, she hoped.

"It's hard to know how to behave in those kinds of circumstances. There's no right or wrong way to support someone," Joan said. "This is kind of the second time pregnancy has come up too. Last time we met up it was more around pregnancy announcements and what it means to be a public figure." Carmen felt certain Joan was deliberately changing the subject, which she was grateful for. She tentatively forked into one of her eggs, letting the runny yolk spill out over the hash browns. Maybe she was a little bit hungry.

"I was thinking about that more, because you're right, it's kind of interesting. We used to define 'public figures' more concretely than we do now. I mean, I think generally it's individuals who have chosen a role or profession that puts them in the public light. And in the past, I think you could make an argument that it generally also meant they were separate in some way, like had the resources to travel separately or have a PR person write them an apology if they said something terrible. Of course, there were probably some exceptions. But now public figure could mean a 19-year old YouTuber who makes less than $30K a year but still has thousands or millions of fans. That's truly a whole different scenario," Joan said.

"Plus, I'm not sure there was as much of a cultural expectation for morality in our public figures," Carmen added. Joan knit her eyebrow together, puzzled. "I mean, we've always wanted people to be good. I don't think there was ever a time we wanted our movie-stars or famous figures to be bad people. But I just think we only heard from them, like them as people, maybe a few times in a year. Or I guess in the old days maybe only a few times in their entire career. You know? But now, that 19-year old YouTuber we hear from her every day. She's bound to say or do something we deem immoral. Or she's bound to not say something we think she should be saying, in a certain way or at a certain time, and that's what we find wrong. And like, we aren't clergy or journalists or politicians. People follow me because they like my clothes. The idea that anyone with a following must chime in on current events feels like it drowns out the people who actually think about that stuff for a living. Not to mention who likely have the resources or educational background to do proper fact checking or whatever," Carmen concluded.

Joan had pulled out her little notebook again, jotting down some things.

"Just a warning, for whatever it's worth, I doubt your listeners will care much about that unless they are influencers themselves," Carmen said.

"You think so? Why? I think it's a pretty interesting cultural phenomenon."

"Well, I'm sure you'd know better than me. It's just, and listen I'm not trying to give you a sob story here or anything, but no one really cares how influencers feel or how we're treated."

"You don't think so?" Joan asked. She seemed sincere. She seemed curious. But Carmen couldn't help but feel a little defeated.

"Well yeah. They think we're dumb. Like, a joke. Even though they spend hours and hours watching us, our careers are still usually a joke to them. Especially how we're portrayed in media, not that it comes up that often or anything. But if they portray a YouTuber or Instagram star as a character in an SNL skit, they are going to portray them as stupid, self-absorbed and probably like a child. So that's one side of it. The other side is we choose this. If you choose to be a public figure, then anything that happens to you is your fault or you just have to put up with it. That's generally the argument," Carmen said.

"But what if you didn't know what you were signing up for?" Joan asked.

Carmen shrugged. "Then you probably quit. I don't know if there are stats out there on how often or quickly people quit influencer careers but I would bet it's high."

"This may be hard to answer but I'd also love to get a sense of the levels of, well, fame or being a public figure. Like, who are the smallest influencers you know who are still doing it as their full-time career? I've seen the term micro influencer thrown around, but I don't know what that means," Joan asked.

"I don't either. Not, like, in a numbers sense. I'm not sure who has the smallest audience but is still making it work, maybe Rosie and Leena? They are in my RTLAS group. Honestly, if you'd ever like to join one of our monthly calls, like if you had some specific questions, I know they'd all like to meet you. I told them when we first met, and they were pretty much all fans of your show."

"Really? OK, that might be cool. Thanks."

"Actually, you know, and I'm just spitballing here. I literally just thought of this and maybe it's a bad idea. I don't know. But AMT has this very active message board where tons of large and small influencers check in to learn more and chat with each other. I bet you could post on there, as yourself, and get tons of responses. I am sure lots of them listen to your show or have heard of it."

"Hmm. I'm not sure. I'll have to think on that more. But thanks for the tip."

This time Joan paid for both their meals, Carmen hadn't even noticed she had slipped their server her card at some point.

"You didn't have to pay. Thank you," Carmen said.

"You've had a shitty week. It doesn't fix anything but it's something. Thanks for meeting with me again. Actually, I was telling my partner, Monica, about our chat last time and she's since been following you. I think she's becoming a fan girl. I like to tease her about it."

Carmen laughed, she was flattered. They said their goodbyes and Carmen walked back to her car across the small parking lot. She sent Leena a quick text before she started driving.

> Thinking about you. If you need anything let me know.

She saw the typing dots flash across the screen then go away. Then a yellow heart emoji appeared with no other text. Carmen sighed and started her car. What else could she do, she wondered? She agreed with Joan, there was no right or wrong way to support someone. But what Leena was going through looked like a heavy boulder to carry and Carmen just wished there was a way she could put it on her back instead, at least for a few hours. Checking in, sending flowers (both of which she'd already done) didn't feel like enough. There had to be something else.

CHAPTER 16

Pam
@freshlystitched

153 POSTS	**32.1K** FOLLOWERS	**2,597** FOLLOWING

Pam reached over and tapped "Snooze" as her phone alarm dinged at her. It was her day off, but she was determined to be productive. She was going to have dinner with Caleb that night, and if he asked what she did all day she didn't want to have to say scrolled the internet, which normally would be true. She instinctively pulled her phone toward her face and opened the Instagram app. It was like making coffee, a normal part of her morning routine.

After a few minutes she rolled over and forced herself up and out of bed. She started making coffee. She cycled through various methods but currently she was into French press again. She had found a vintage French press the last time she had been thrifting and it reignited her love for the method. It was probably from the 1960s or 1970s, it was made of amber glass and looked like something straight out of *Mad Men*. She thought about who else might have owned it before her as she added her grounds and slowly filled it with piping hot water. She loved old things. She didn't understand people who didn't. Plus, it was better for the environment, to reuse things that were already here rather than buying new all the time. Not to mention, who had the funds to do that?

While she sipped her coffee, she checked her shop messages (only one) and printed off a few mailing labels. She was shipping a couple orders off today. She had started a new project where people could mail her their old family quilts, ones they had from grandmothers or great-grandmothers usually, and she'd turn them into other things like Christmas stockings or oven-mitt sets. She'd gotten a flood of orders when she announced it and had to limit the number she took on, as most of them wanted Christmas stockings so the window of time to complete them and mail them back was small. The response had surprised her, and at first, she had been intimidated once the quilts started to arrive. She worried she'd ruin a family heirloom or mix up the orders somehow and make the wrong quilt into someone else's order. But that hadn't happened. And it had actually been really fun working with these used quilts. It made her feel like she was giving new life to something that already existed, rather than making something new. She sort of hated participating in capitalism at all but being adjacent to the slow-fashion movement felt good. It was her own small protest. She was happy when she could find those little wins. Maybe she wasn't saving the world or changing the minds of millions, but she was doing something. Perhaps it didn't matter, and it was all just a vanity project for her to feel like she was doing something. Who knew?

Coffee only filled her for so long, so she decided to make some toast. She had bought a loaf of sourdough bread at work. Apparently Carla, Al's wife, had gotten into sourdough starters and baking bread. She was gearing up to join the farmer's market and had brought a bunch of loaves in to work, half priced. Sourdough starter was a pretty fascinating substance, not too different from taking care of plants really. Just another organism that needed things from you, but sourdough starter gave back. Well, if you were willing to bake it did, anyway. She sliced off two thick pieces and shoved them in her ancient toaster, they emerged moments later nearly burnt. Exactly how she liked toast. The almost smoky smell filling her little kitchen. She slathered on some butter, honey, and sprinkles of flaky sea salt on top. She scrolled as she chewed. Her account had added nearly three hundred new followers since she had announced the heirloom quilt project. Not bad.

The rest of her morning and afternoon went by without a hitch. She mailed off her orders and baked some brownies to take over to Caleb's that night. He was making her dinner, so she thought she'd arrive to his place with wine and chocolate in the form of homemade brownies. She was no Suzy-homemaker, but sometimes she liked to bake. A package arrived, which she tentatively opened. It was a vintage door handle, with a lock that she had bought off eBay. It looked similar to the other door knobs in her old house, but none of her interior doors had locks. She pulled out the miscellaneous tools she had in her closet and found a YouTube video about replacing door knobs. She followed the instructions and with only a few minor hiccups she had installed the new (old) door handle to her studio room. Ever since Caleb had seen the crib she had in her sewing studio, she had wanted to make the space a little more private. She hoped Caleb would be over again, maybe even other friends—although she hadn't had anyone inside her house for what felt like years (maybe it was?). But she wanted her sewing studio to be her space, and so a lock on the door seemed like a good idea.

She parked her car in the steep driveway of Caleb's house. It looked a little bigger than hers and quite a bit newer, but way less charming. The neighborhood was quiet. No one was out walking and only a few houses sported any kind of leftover seasonal décor. The complete opposite of her neighborhood. She hoped she had the right house. She checked the address he'd sent her against the numbers on the mailbox. Just then the front door opened, and Caleb stepped out. He waved to her. She waved back.

"What's this?" he asked, pointing to the glass Tupperware she carried. She held it up along with the bottle of wine in her other hand.

"I come bearing gifts," she said. "I made brownies and brought wine. I felt kind of bad that you were making everything, and I wanted to contribute."

"I love it. Please come in," he said as he held the door wide for her. Unlike his impromptu introduction to her place, he had known she was coming. Everything was clean and picked up. He took the brownies and wine from her and set them on the counter before giving her a little tour of the house. The living and kitchen area were an open concept, and then there were two bedrooms. One was his and the other was filled with plants and a terrarium. He had a pet tarantula, which was news to Pam. She jumped when she saw it, crawling up the side of its enclosure.

"That's Ruby. She's been with me for nine years. You'll have to win her approval if you're going to stick around," he joked. Pam just stared at the furry creature.

"How long do they typically live for? I honestly know nothing about them."

"I get it. I can tell by your face you're a little freaked out. First of all, they don't bite. Well, they don't bite people. Or at least that's super rare. Maybe if you scared her," he explained. Pam just stared at the tank. "And males live around ten years, but females like my Ruby here can live as long as 30 years. So, we're still just getting to know each other."

"Wow. That's a long time," was all she could think to say.

"Honestly, I think of her as one of the plants. Of course, she's not; she thinks and feels much more than any of my plants. Not that she tells me any of it. But I guess I think of her as the caretaker of the space. She's the shepherd of the plants, plus she loves warmth just like the plants so it's a good relationship," Caleb said as he thankfully led them back toward the kitchen. Pam decided she would just put it out of her mind that there was a giant spider in the other room. She did not like that spider, but she liked Caleb. Maybe she could just forget about Ruby.

"Well, what are we having? And does it go well with Cab?" she asked, looking around for a wine opener. Caleb handed her one from a drawer.

"I'm making chicken fried rice, which is one of the main meals I can make well. I also thought we could make spring rolls to go with it."

Pam now noticed that he had all the ingredients for fresh spring rolls laid out on the counter, down to a little plate with water for moistening the wrappers.

"Wow. I'm impressed."

"Really? That's exactly what I was hoping," he said with a smile. Pam sipped her wine. Focus on that smile, she told herself, forget about the spider.

They got to work, wetting the spring roll wrappers, filling them, and rolling them up. The first few were either too full (and busted) or too loose and kind of resembled pulled-off condom wrappers. Or party balloons, but the party was now over. But then they got the hang of it.

Caleb's kitchen was small, so they were almost on top of each other as they worked. They had nearly finished the bottle of wine she brought by the time they sat down to eat. Caleb opened a second bottle and offered to top off her glass. She nodded yes.

"So, what did you do with yourself today? I know it was your day off because I was at work."

"Just random errands and little things around the house mostly. I shipped a few orders from my shop, that kind of thing," she explained. She didn't want to bore him with the details.

"Oh yeah. How is the heirloom quilt thing going? I saw your post. Looked like such a cool idea." She had forgotten he started following her shop account. She was surprised he had noticed. Her ex never would have paid attention to something like that. Not that she should compare them to each other, she reminded herself.

"Yeah, actually that's been really popular. I had to stop taking orders or it would have been too many for me to handle," she said.

"Nice. Do you ever want to do just that? Your shop? And like, stop working at the greenhouse or maybe scale back to part time? Your account is so big, it would probably be easy."

"That's nice of you to say but I don't know. I'm not sure I could. The work I do for my shop is pretty labor intensive. It would be hard to take on enough to pay my bills, even if it was there. And I'm proud of my little following but it's actually pretty small compared to people who do that kind of thing as their job."

"Why not charge more for your work?" he asked. As if it was that simple. Just a basic math problem.

"Well, I could. But I don't know if that's right. It's a little capitalistic, don't you think?"

"So is our society. You have to play by the rules of the game or don't play at all. Or lose, I guess."

"I don't agree. I think if something seems immoral to you then you can choose your own rules to play by," she said. Maybe it came out a little harsher than she intended. She should probably pump the brakes on the wine.

"I get what you're saying. I do. But I also think if the other Etsy shops start charging more and you don't, then you're the only one getting punished and it's by your own hand. How is that fair?"

"Sometimes it's costly to have principles," she said. For a few moments Caleb just stared at her. She wondered if he was upset.

"What are you thinking?" she asked.

"I was just picturing you in the Batman suit. Pretty sexy visual."

Pam laughed so hard she nearly spit out her wine. "I'm probably more of a Poison Ivy type. You know, being a plant-lady and all."

"Well, me too then. I'm a total Poison Ivy," he said with a laugh.

Maybe it was the wine. Maybe it was the delicious dinner, or the fact that he'd made spring rolls with her. Maybe it was how he knew and cared about her hobby, how he asked about her day and seemed to actually want to know the answer. Or maybe it was the wine. But Pam leaned over and kissed him, really kissed him. Caleb kissed her back. They both tasted like red wine and peanut sauce and neither of them cared.

"Would you like to move to the couch?" he asked between kisses. She nodded. She nearly dragged him, pulled him down on her when they got there. He followed her lead. She pulled his shirt off, and he let her. Then she pulled hers off too. That was the go signal Caleb had apparently been waiting for because then the gloves were off. He undid her bra and kissed her breasts. She wished the lights were dimmer, she'd always been embarrassed of her cherry moles and freckles. If he noticed he either didn't care or loved them. She moved to unbutton his pants and that's when he stopped for a moment and looked at her, really looked at her. She felt self-conscious, being half naked.

"What? Is this OK?" she asked.

"I'm, well. We've both been drinking. Do you want to stop? We can just watch something, you can stay over if you don't feel good to drive and there is no obligation. None," he said, a little breathless. She smiled.

"I would like to stay over. But I'd like to have sex with you if you're up for it Caleb?" Pam was shocked to see a deep red blush blossom over his face. It made him look at least five years younger, it was adorable. And with that she led him into his bedroom, careful not to look Ruby's way as she did.

CHAPTER 17

Joan
@thisisnow_podcast

618 POSTS | **55.8K** FOLLOWERS | **56** FOLLOWING

Joan followed Monica as they hiked toward the Griffith Observatory. Monica had suggested they start hiking together once a week, since they now drove everywhere instead of walking like they had in Brooklyn. It had been a great suggestion, especially once Joan checked her phone's health app and saw her steps per day had plummeted since their move. But now she regretted it, trudging up a steep hill with a number of other Angelenos around them in matching lululemon sets. Joan didn't mind being cliché, but she was more out of shape than she'd realized. The only good part of the hike so far was her partner was consistently ahead of her, and Monica had a great ass.

"Some of my coworkers started doing this walk on our lunch break," Monica explained. She was a veterinarian, now almost a vet's assistant but she'd work her way back up. Their office was at the base of this hike, so they had parked there.

"Don't you get all sweaty?" Joan asked. "Or is it just me who's now grossly out of shape?"

Monica smiled. "You want to know a secret?" she asked as she cast her eyes around, making sure their fellow hikers weren't too close. "We rinse off in the dog wash. It's a little awkward but it works," she said with a wink. Joan could only imagine. And she did, so she laughed.

"How's the influencer story idea going? I saw Carmen posted about being in Houston a couple weeks ago."

Joan had to nearly pant a few breaths in and out before she could answer. God this hill was steep. She explained, without too much detail as it felt somewhat private, what had happened to Carmen's friend Leena. And how they had discussed pregnancy announcements the first time, and then miscarriages the next. Monica was still a few steps ahead of her on the path, but Joan could see her shoulders drop in empathy at the story. They hadn't talked much more about trying to have a kid since that first time, and Joan worried this conversation would depress Monica. Or give her the impression that Joan was already giving up.

"Maybe that should be the story," Monica said after a few beats. The crunch of the gravel beneath their feet was the only sound for a moment.

"What? A woman having a miscarriage?" Joan asked.

"No, just all of it. Pregnancy, navigating that. Miscarriage, navigating that. Motherhood, navigating that," she said, then added, "Also, not wanting to have children and what that's like. In some ways the story would probably be about what it's like to be an adult woman. Once our periods arrive, fertility and motherhood—or the lack of it or the inability to do it—start to define our lives without us even knowing or wanting it. You're either not wanting to be a mother, and the burden of birth control usually falls to you unless you're one of us lucky lesbians. Or you want to be a mother, and I'm sure that has its own pains and complications like trying to get pregnant and then miscarriages. And most of that falls on women's shoulders too. And then motherhood, that's a big change in women's lives as well. Certainly, it becomes the thing we define women by once they are mothers."

"Hmm," Joan said, thinking. Also catching her breath again. "I don't hate it. It's sort of a big leap from my original idea, but everyone I've met so far is still a part of this too, which is kind of interesting. I have to admit though, I don't know if I feel like the right person to put together this kind of piece. I identify as a woman, sure. But I think my sexual orientation and maybe my looks or personality, I don't know, kind of put me on the outside of this discussion in some ways. Like, I don't think I felt many of the pressures you just described."

"Maybe that makes you the perfect person to do it?" Monica pointed out.

They had finally reached a summit point with an amazing view and one small bench. Joan headed for the bench and unscrewed her water bottle top, drinking deeply. Monica sat beside her.

"I still like the influencer idea too. It just feels like this might be leading you somewhere else and I think you should follow."

"I like it when a story leads me. Feels like I'm uncovering a fossil," Joan said.

"Oh! I could see you as an archeologist. Sexy. Maybe you should be one for Halloween, I could be a dinosaur," Monica teased. Joan loved that she was constantly thinking about Halloween, even when the season had just ended. It was cute. And in that moment, maybe the endorphins from the hike were flooding her brain, but she felt an overwhelming sense of gratitude for her partner. She still didn't know how she felt about having a kid, but she hoped somewhere inside she wanted it too so that Monica could have that. Maybe changing the focus of this story would help her learn more about that part of life.

Maybe this was the universe's way of helping her little journalist heart to explore that possibility.

Joan was running late. She hated being late, even if she messaged ahead. Her video window popped open in the chat, the other four women from the RTLAS group already there. Leena had been speaking, she was clearly crying so she was probably in the middle of telling the rest of the women the story Carmen had told Joan. Interrupting a story like that made it even worse that she was late to the call. Great.

"Please, continue, I'll introduce myself after. Sorry again," she mumbled as she clicked her mute button, making it clear she wanted Leena to continue and she would be silent. Even though Carmen had told Joan the story already, there were more details from Leena's account. The bit about a package arriving and it being a baby blanket made the story that much sadder, now the blanket just sat in her bedroom as a painful reminder.

"And I haven't felt up to sharing much about it online, but it's getting to a point where I think I need to say something. Every time I post about a recipe I get at least a couple comments asking how I'm doing with the pregnancy, if I'm having cravings, that sort of thing. They mean well but it makes me cry every time. And my campaign is about to start, with the coconut milk series, so I just want to get the news out there, so I can move on and not have to worry about it as I start sharing more work," Leena concluded.

"Not to be a wet blanket but you probably will still get a few comments here and there, even after you share what happened," Carmen said.

"I know. There's no perfect solution. But I think a lot of people will give me space if I ask for it," Leena said. The group seemed to agree. Joan now took note of each of the women and the backgrounds of their videos. She had already looked them all up online and was familiar with what they looked like and what kind of content they made. But she got to see little glimpses of their homes or the coffee shop they were in, and it was interesting. She noticed Rosie, who she knew was pregnant, was sitting in a room in her house with a lot of boxes behind her. Joan could see one of them had a picture of a crib on it. There were baby toys, books, and a quilt sitting on top. Maybe she'd just had her baby shower and was still unpacking. This miscarriage story from her friend Leena must freak her out on a lot of levels, Joan thought.

"Anyway, let's hear from our guest," Leena said, wiping her eyes. She seemed ready to change the subject and Joan couldn't blame her. She unmuted her screen.

"Yes, hi. I'm Joan. I host the podcast *This Is Now*. And Carmen invited me to meet you all and sit in on one of your calls. So, thank you. This is probably obvious already but I'm not recording anything, although I may take some notes. I'm still exploring ideas for this story."

"We all love your show," said Rosie.

"It's true. Tell us more about what you think the story is so far," said Abby.

"Well, to be honest, I am considering taking it in another direction," she could see Carmen's eyebrows raise slightly, as Joan hadn't even had the chance to tell her this yet. "I try to follow a story, wherever it takes me once I'm in it. I try not to have preconceived ideas or a conclusion I'm already working toward as that can limit what I see. I'm thinking about doing a piece on the role of motherhood in the lives of women. Women who want children. Women who have lost children or had a miscarriage. Women who can't have children. Women who have children and how it changes and defines their lives and career. And women who don't want children, and how that becomes a defining label for them." Joan could see the women were taking this in and feeling apprehensive. She continued, "I'm not planning to use any of your stories, unless you allow me to. As I said, I'm still just gathering ideas."

The women just sat in their little screens for a moment, clearly a little unsure what to say. Joan hadn't even realized it until this moment, but this group represented most of the groups she was looking for: a current mother, someone wanting and waiting to become one, one who had a miscarriage, and one who didn't want children at all. It felt as if this fact dawned on the members of the group too, sort of an uncomfortable realization given Leena had just shared her story.

"Well. If you want my vote, it sounds like it might be kind of boring. I probably wouldn't click on an episode that had the word motherhood in the title," Carmen admitted. The other women rolled their eyes, a few with shouts of 'Carmen' as if she'd just booed a performer.

"What? I'm just being honest. I'm not trying to be rude or anything," Carmen said, the edges of her mouth turning up in a smile. Joan was just glad she wasn't mad at the change of direction. As if Joan had tricked her into getting into this group.

"It might be boring. I think that's very possible," Joan said. "I also think it's kind of a polarizing subject, which is interesting to me because it affects pretty much all women in one way or another."

"Like you can't escape being defined by it, positively or negatively," Abby said. As the veteran mom of the group, she probably got it in all sorts of ways, Joan thought.

"OK, this is random," Rosie began, "But my friend Jackie, she's a doctor. She just had a miscarriage and she told me she sent her fetus off to the lab to learn more about what happened. Also, I guess I should say she's an OB/GYN. And although I'm sure she can't talk about any patients specifically, for confidentiality reasons and all that, she has a really unique and deep perspective on pregnancy and miscarriage. She's also one of the strongest and most interesting women I know. She's not an influencer but if your story is changing she might be someone you'd want to connect with," Rosie offered.

"Wow, that is an interesting perspective," Joan said as she jotted some notes. "I've met a few medical professionals before for other stories and they always have something very valuable to say," Joan hesitated before she continued, "Do you know if she got the, um, results back yet?"

Rosie seemed to gulp at this. But she answered, "I know she got the results, but I don't know what they were. She'd know better than me. Plus, we don't get to meet up super often, since she's really busy. And, well, I guess now that she's had a miscarriage and I'm still pregnant I feel weird meeting up. Like my body, my bump, will remind her of her loss." Joan chanced a glance at Leena's video window, her dark skin looked pale and she didn't look up.

"You're based in Kansas City, right?" Joan asked Rosie.

"Yep. Born and raised."

"And your friend, Jackie, is there too?"

"Yes. She works at the University of Kansas hospital," Rosie said.

"I'm actually going to be in KC next week, for a different story. Maybe that's too short of notice, but do you think you could put me in touch with her? It would be nice to meet in person, rather than over the phone," Joan explained.

"Sure, yeah. I can do that," Rosie said. Joan could feel a slight hesitation in her answer.

"And if she's busy, or just doesn't want to meet, or thinks this story idea sounds as boring as Carmen does I promise I won't be pushy," Joan said. Rosie smiled.

"I said it might be boring. Might. Get my quotes right, I thought you were a journalist," Carmen said with mock anger. The entire group laughed, including Leena.

CHAPTER 18

Ela
@justanotherela

58 POSTS	**599** FOLLOWERS	**832** FOLLOWING

E la had been sewing. A lot. And the new projects had been fun, but it wasn't the fulfilling sort of work she had been hoping for. She knew she needed to find her higher purpose. It felt like it was right around the corner, her new season of life was about to begin.

She finished the piece she was working on, pulled the fabric away from the machine and cut the threads. Out of habit she pulled out her phone and began to scroll. She had finally started a new account for work stuff, but she still used her personal account as her kind of junk food account. She consumed celebrity gossip and kept up with the latest Vlogger to get canceled along with videos of baby pigs and otters. Since she never posted on her personal account anymore and had deleted most of what was on it, she also used it to leave whatever comments she felt like. It was the closest to being anonymous you could get on Instagram.

Ela saw one of her favorite follows had a new post. She had somehow missed it. It was a photo of the woman standing outside, the sun streaming golden light behind her and she was holding a sonogram photo and smiling wide. *Oh god*, thought Ela, *another one*. It felt like everyone she followed was getting pregnant. The caption read: 'So excited to become a mother soon, we could not be happier!!!' It was a fairly harmless announcement, but Ela could feel a few hot tears building behind her eyes. She couldn't escape anywhere. Even when all she needed was a break or a place to calm down and stop spiraling, she couldn't. It was always ruined by shit like this.

She saw the post already had seven hundred comments and had been posted a few days ago. She scrolled through the comments, which were 95% things like, 'so happy for you' and 'congratulations.' But then she saw one comment that had started a longer thread that she resonated with. The user's name was @Mj_1985 and they had typed: "Congrats to you but do keep in mind that some of us are struggling with things like infertility or loss and it's hard to see posts like this pop up in our feed all the time." After that another commenter had said "Agree with @Mj_1989 It's hard to be excited for you when you clearly haven't thought about how your news will impact others." And then another comment after which simply said, "Be happy for her or leave. You don't have to make her news about yourself." And then the comments spiraled from there.

Ela read through them all and decided enough was enough. She had seen these internet arguments over and over. She had participated in many herself, which mostly just got her blocked. She felt a little disappointed that someone she had truly thought was cool had fallen into the same category as everyone else. So cliché. Had she even considered an alternative? But whatever, it was always the same. Nothing new or that Ela hadn't seen a million times already. And even though she had seen these arguments, had these arguments, many times before, today it clicked. She had been formulating a plan for a while.

She had even put parts of it into action, but then had chickened out. But not today. Today was the first day of her new destiny. She was going to change the world in the way she knew she was meant to.

She was careful as she added items to the box, adding extra bio-degradable packing peanuts so nothing would crack or break during shipping. She carefully taped up the package and used her non-dom-inant hand to write the address. She didn't want credit. As she looked at the small box sitting by her front door, ready to be sent off, she felt good. She decided to go ahead and pack up a few more boxes.

CHAPTER 19

Jackie
@docjackie

| **106** POSTS | **328** FOLLOWERS | **452** FOLLOWING |

Jackie pulled into the parking lot of the wine bar that was only two blocks away from her new neighborhood. They were still unpacking, but she'd been to this bar a few times already. It was never very busy, so the location and the privacy made it seem like a good place to suggest to the podcaster to meet up. Jackie was actually a little excited. She'd been listening to *This Is Now*, jumping around to episodes that seemed interesting, ever since Rosie had asked to share her email with Joan. She realized in all her years as a medical professional she'd never once been interviewed for anything, not that she'd expected to. But still, this was something new and a little exciting. It had been nice to have something to look forward to. She'd been in a heavy funk for a while. She knew it would pass, but she'd been surprised how heavy life had felt ever since the event. The pathology report hadn't helped at all.

As she walked into the dark, velveted booth bar, she saw an attractive woman sitting at the bar alone. Something about the way she carried herself, all that confidence, made Jackie think this must be her. She caught her eye and the woman nodded a hello. Jackie headed her way.

"Hi, I'm Joan. Thank you for meeting with me. And thank you for suggesting such a fun spot. I'm always excited to find little local gems when I travel, and this feels like something probably only this neighborhood knows about."

Jackie beamed. She might work 60+ hour weeks but she still knew a few cute spots apparently.

"I'm Jackie. Yes, I live not too far from here. We recently moved to this neighborhood and although I haven't explored too much yet, I did immediately like this place."

Joan signaled to the bartender that they were going to move to a booth. Then she led Jackie, taking her half-drank glass of red wine with her. As they sat down, the server, in heavy black eyeliner, asked for Jackie's order.

"I'll have whatever she's having," she said. She hadn't had a chance to look at the menu and red wine sounded great. The server looked to Joan who said, "It's a cab. I think it was the cheapest one you had by the glass," and smiled sheepishly. Jackie giggled as the server walked off to get her drink. She hadn't expected humor and humility, although she wasn't sure why not.

"I hope you like it," Joan said.

"Honestly, I wouldn't know the difference."

"Clearly, me neither," Joan said with a wide smile. The wine had made the inside of her lips just a little bit pink. It was kind of cute. It reminded Jackie of college days, which felt like lifetimes ago.

"So, you're doing a story about miscarriage, and you want my unique perspective as a doctor and a woman who's recently had one." Jackie said. Joan just stared. "I'm just breaking the ice all the way. We've got some deep ground to cover if so."

"Yes. That is what I want to talk about. But, and I mean this sincerely, only what you want to share. And if there are things you want to share but you want 'off the record' that's OK too. I'm just gathering data still at this point and I realize how personal and painful this subject may be. Well, actually I don't have any idea how painful it is truly. I've never had a miscarriage. But I don't want to be insensitive," Joan explained. The server had brought Jackie's glass of wine, and she took a big drink.

"Well, where should I start? Do you want to hear about what miscarriage is from a medical perspective, the current stats on how likely and often they occur? I don't know there's a lot I could say I guess," Jackie said.

"Why don't you tell me your story first. However, much you want to share. Rosie told me you had a miscarriage, but she didn't share any details with me, so I'd really like to hear you tell it."

Jackie surprised herself as she felt a few tears well up at the front of her eyes. She also realized it might feel really good to tell the whole story, maybe it would feel like a release. She steeled herself and told Joan the whole story: looking at the new house and thinking of raising their kid there, the bath and feeling ill, waiting for the ambulance alone but knowing something was wrong, and making the decision to send the fetus to pathology. She felt a few tears leak out as she told the story of that terrible night, but overall, she held it together. Joan just listened intently. "It's weird you mention taking a bath, another woman who just told me her miscarriage story said she also took a bath just before. I don't know why that stands out to me, but it does," Joan said.

"I even used a bath bomb, which I never buy things like that. I'm normally not much of a bath person."

"This might seem weird, but where did you get the bath bomb? Do you remember where you bought it?"

"I didn't. Actually, it's funny, I got it from Rosie. She gets lots of little gifts and things in PR boxes or from fans. She'd hate me saying this, but she's pretty famous in her world and she gets a surprising amount of fan gifts." Joan made a few notes in a little notepad she had.

"And, do many women send their fetus to pathology after an event like this? I guess I hadn't realized this was an option at all. But I'm not very familiar with the world of fertility and birth, I will admit," Joan said.

"I wouldn't say many women do. It is an option, maybe not every hospital has it, but most teaching hospitals do. Probably it's because it's kind of a delicate thing to bring up once a woman has had a miscarriage. It also depends on how it has occurred. Like, what shape the fetus is in, how much tissue there is to test, those kind of factors," Jackie explained.

"And, did you get the results? Anything you are OK sharing?"

"I did get the results, although I've sent off for additional testing. The results are hard to explain as they didn't make much sense to me or to any of my colleagues I've consulted. The easiest way to explain it is it seemed like the fetus had a severe allergic reaction to something, almost like it was poisoned. But we also can't rule out all genetic factors, it could have to do with a chromosome defect in combination with an outside element that caused the appearance of this allergic reaction. If it's a genetic or chromosome issue I would want to know more, as it could happen again with other pregnancies. So, that's why I'm waiting on more lab results."

"Are you allergic to anything? Did you also feel like you were having an allergic reaction, or had been poisoned?" Joan asked.

"I'm not allergic to anything that I know of. I felt very ill, but it came on pretty quickly. I felt fine most of the day, but then after my bath I started feeling ill and then it all happened within a matter of 30 minutes. So, I guess in that sense it felt more like poisoning. I've only ever experienced food poisoning, which I would compare it to in how quickly it came on. But with food poisoning you can usually guess or at least narrow down what it may have been. Bad chicken, something along those lines, right? This didn't have a clear cause at all."

Joan wrote down more notes in her notebook. Both women had ordered another glass of wine. Joan moved the conversation along to less personal matters, asking about both the stats and her own experiences as a doctor with how often miscarriage occurs, pregnancy and birth generally, and postpartum recovery and depression. She was starting to feel like the story was maybe not too boring, as Carmen has said, but maybe too dark. She'd reported on murders before, but this was on another level and it was happening all the time. It was oddly common.

"Don't take this the wrong way, but do you think your story will also focus on the good parts of having a child?" Jackie asked. There was no judgment in her voice, but Joan felt the accusation all the same.

"I'd like the story to be about, well, what it's like to be a woman and how our biology inevitably defines us. I'd like to present it as both an oppressive and inescapable force but also the beauty and meaning of having children when one chooses to and is able," Joan said. Jackie looked skeptical.

"Maybe that didn't sound reassuring. My partner, Monica, wants to have children. So, I guess I also have to admit that I'm feeling somewhat drawn to this subject as a journalist because it's drawing me in both personally and professionally. I don't want to get too woo-woo on you, but it feels like the universe is trying to tell me something. I don't know what it is yet. But I feel like I'm on the path I'm supposed to walk down," Joan said. She hadn't even realized how true this was until she said it out loud.

"Well, I hope you find what you're supposed to find," Jackie said. Joan smiled back and picked up the check.

Joan thanked Jackie as the two rose to leave. Jackie said she could email her anytime, she liked the show a lot and was proud to help in any way she could. This meant a lot to Joan.

As Joan got into her rental car she couldn't shake the eerie feeling she'd gotten from hearing Jackie's story. The bath and bath bomb were the same as Leena's story. What if the bath bomb was the 'bad chicken' that caused the miscarriage? The hypothesis sounded ridiculous, even to Joan. But she couldn't get it off her mind. Sometimes products did get pulled off shelves after they had been sold. Maybe a chemical in a fragrance? It could be possible. Also, maybe a too hot bath? But Jackie was a doctor, and she would know if something like that could affect an early pregnancy. Surely she would have mentioned it. Before she overthought too much, she texted Carmen about the AMT message board she had mentioned. By the time Joan was pulling into her hotel parking lot, Carmen had already texted back with the details of how to set up an account and log on.

She sat on her hotel bed and pulled out her laptop. She set up another email box just for this purpose, in case she had a lot of weird messages, which seemed likely. Then she created her account on the AMT site and added her message to the general board, it read:

I'm Joan, the host of the This Is Now *podcast. I'm doing a story about pregnancy, birth, miscarriage, and motherhood. I'm not very far along in my research, but I'm starting to hear*

what a pattern could be, so I wanted to ask a larger group.
Here's my request: if you have had a miscarriage in the last
few years AND it happened shortly after you had a bath and
used scented products of any kind, I'd love to hear your story.
Please email me at: dearjoan@thisisnow.com. You are wel-
come to stay anonymous and please know I would not share
your story on an episode without contacting you first.

She had decided not to mention bath bombs specifically, as she wanted to see if it would come up organically. She posted the message and
immediately felt stupid. She read over it again and it sounded almost
like a conspiracy theory. She had to be on the wrong path. But she
couldn't move on until she found out for sure.

Joan changed and brushed her teeth and washed her face. She looked
at her reflection, her slightly red complexion and few fine lines that
seemed to be deepening this year. Maybe it was time to have a kid
with Monica. She didn't want to wait until she was too old to enjoy
it all and keep up with chasing a toddler around. Plus, what if they
had to go through a lot before they even gave birth? Maybe Monica
would consider adoption more; it felt safer in some ways.

It had been less than 20 minutes since Joan had posted to the message board. On a whim she decided to check the inbox she had set
up before closing her laptop and going to bed. She already had four
messages, one with the subject line that read 'why I can't use bath
bombs anymore.'

CHAPTER 20

Joan
@thisisnow_podcast

612 POSTS | **54.6K** FOLLOWERS | **56** FOLLOWING

J oan had received over 200 emails overnight. It was astounding. She wondered if this group, for some reason, had a higher incidence of miscarriage than the general public. And if so, why? She had begun sorting them into two groups before responding. Well, three groups really. Group one was those who had a miscarriage and specifically mentioned taking a bath with a bath bomb. Group two were those who had miscarriages but didn't mention bath bombs (some did mention things like bubble bath, or a new-scent soap they had just started using, but not specifically bath bombs). And the third group were those who hadn't had a miscarriage but knew someone who did and seemed to have a story about a bath. This third group Joan completely ignored for the time being, as she had enough to sort through already.

Group one emails were the ones she was most interested in. There were an astonishing 24 women in this group. She thought the fact that so many specifically mentioned bath bombs, even when her message had not used this term, was too much of a coincidence to ignore. She tried never to let her mind jump to conclusions when she worked, she didn't want to get tunnel vision and miss something. But she couldn't help but wonder if maybe there was a certain essential oil that had been in the bath bombs, or some kind of ingredient that could possibly cause premature birth. This group did seem to use essential oils more than the average. She also wondered if there was some manufacturer that was producing toxic bath bombs and didn't know—or did but didn't care or didn't have the safeguards in place to correct the issue. What if this product was still on the shelves somewhere, maybe more women would have miscarriages until Joan got to the bottom of this. Who knew? Her mind raced even though she tried to stop it.

She systematically wrote back to each of the women in group one. She offered condolences, of course. And she asked questions, taking care not to be too leading. She often asked questions that were completely unrelated, not wanting to make it too clear what she was looking for. But she did ask if they remembered where they had bought the bath bombs, or what scent they had been, among other questions. She offered to call if they'd rather talk than email. She reminded them they could stay anonymous. And she wouldn't share their story or record them without their consent.

Writing back just to these initial emails had taken most of her day. Soon she would have to pack up and head to the airport to make her evening flight. Joan startled as her cell phone buzzed beneath her leg on the bed. She saw Monica's name flash across the screen as she picked up.

"Hey there, beautiful. Just calling to say I miss you and I can't wait for you to get home later tonight. Trip going OK?" Monica asked.

"Yeah, you could say that," Joan said. Then she explained what she had learned from Jackie the night before and from posting on the message board. Monica gasped when she heard the number of women who had mentioned bath bombs in their miscarriage stories.

"Sorry. That just sounds like a LOT. But I'm no journalist. Does that seem, I don't know, possible to you? As in, it's possible they aren't related at all?" Monica asked.

"It seems too odd. But, I don't know yet. I've written them all back, and I imagine it will take at least a week to hear back from them all, if they all even write back. Plus, more emails are still coming in. I have four that arrived in the inbox since you called. It's just wild," Joan said. The journalist side of her was thrilled so many people were reaching out, but another side of her felt like she was seeing a monster's shadow. It was terrifying and sad. She felt her phone vibrate by her ear. She saw Carmen was calling.

"Hey Mon, Carmen is calling me. Do you mind if I take it?"

"Not at all. I love you. See you tonight," Monica said.

"Love you too," Joan tapped to end her call and answer Carmen's. She had barely said hello when she heard Carmen butt in.

"What do you think you're doing exactly?" Carmen said.

"What do you mean?"

"Leena saw your posting on the AMT board. Are you talking about her? She didn't say you could share her story. She's really upset. It feels like you're taunting her, using her story to connect with others for whatever this piece is you're writing."

"No, it's not like that. I…" Joan couldn't finish before Carmen cut her off again.

"I wouldn't be so upset if you were using something I'd said to benefit yourself. But I invited you into my group and it feels like you're taking advantage of Leena. She doesn't deserve that. She's been through a lot."

"I understand. And I promise it's not like that," Joan said.

"Then what is it like? Explain it to me," Carmen demanded. So, Joan filled her in about how Jackie's story had been eerily similar to Leena's, even though they didn't know each other and had never swapped stories. This had prompted Joan to make the message board posting. She shared how many responses she'd gotten so far, and how many more felt like the exact same story as Leena's and Jackie's. Carmen didn't have anything to say for a few beats, which was unlike her.

"So, you think they are related somehow?" Carmen asked.

"I don't know yet. It feels like something, and I'm trying to chase it down. It could be nothing. But I promise I didn't use Leena's story to get more interviews. I think it's possible that Leena, Jackie, and a lot of other women could be victims. Maybe there's a toxic ingredient, like some corporate oversight or something. It's possible the miscarriages happened for a common reason. Maybe. But again, I don't know yet."

"But I don't get it. Leena got her bath bombs in the mail. I think it was a gift from a reader. So, what? You think some asshole sends poisonous bath bombs in the mail? That would be incredibly fucked up. Plus, probably easy to track them," Carmen said, clearly skeptical but Joan could feel the wheels starting to turn in her mind. It was the same thing Joan felt, that this was crazy but also she couldn't stop. And something Jackie had said the night before flashed into Joan's mind.

"Jackie said she got the bath bomb from Rosie. That it had been from a fan or a PR box or whatever. She said the exact same thing you're saying just last night," Joan exclaimed.

"You think Rosie was the target, but Jackie got her bath bomb and happened to be pregnant too, so she had a miscarriage instead?

Wow. Don't say this to Rosie until you are SURE. That's really, well, dark. I don't know how Rosie could live with that kind of guilt," Carmen pointed out. Joan immediately saw how she was right. She had to be sure, or at least 99% sure. But how was she going to do that?

Joan continued to correspond with the women who answered her posting. Some emailed, some wanted to talk. She made time for all of them. At times she felt more like a grief counselor than a journalist. She listened to so many women cry over the phone, it gutted her. She'd interviewed people who had cried before but nothing on this scale. She felt exhausted at the end of every day. Monica knew why and made dinner, gave her space, and chose a light-hearted show for them to watch after dinner without asking. She quietly supported Joan; she was the person handing the marathon runner a cup of water when they felt they couldn't quite go on.

One evening Monica walked through the door, home from work. Their small house was quiet.

"Hey Joan, you home? Any preferences for dinner? I might order out," she called into the house. She heard no reply, but she did hear the sound of papers being shuffled in the living room. She walked through and found Joan with a giant bulletin board taped to the wall, a map of the United States on it with little dots and post-it notes spread out.

"What's this?" Monica asked. Joan startled, as if hearing her for the first time.

"Sorry. I've started to feel really overwhelmed with the number of responses I've gotten. I wanted to organize everything and one way I wanted to look at the data is by where everyone is located. Since everyone I've been talking to is an influencer they are all online, obviously, but I wanted to see where in the US they are located visually. I'm also adding notes for the month and year of their miscarriage, their blog or Instagram name, their follower count, what subjects they cover. I'm just trying to find any sort of pattern, or anything that might connect them further."

Monica took in the map. There were a lot of little pin dots and post it notes scattered throughout but concentrated on the coasts and cities that were more heavily populated. There were two that were off the map completely, she assumed these must be the international cases Joan had told her about. It was a sad monument. And as far as Monica could see, there didn't seem to be any real pattern emerging. The dates indicated they were all within a 3-year timeframe. But other than that, there wasn't much that connected them beyond the obvious. She walked closer to get a better view of the notes and other items Joan had added to the board. One had some kind of medical report taped to it, she tapped it with her finger in question.

"Another woman sent her fetus to pathology, just like Jackie. Apparently, her husband is a doctor, so she knew to do this and felt it would be beneficial. She emailed me the results, but they don't make much sense to me. I already forwarded them on to Jackie, with the woman's permission to share them with another doctor. I'm waiting to hear back what she thinks," Joan said.

"What are these?" Monica asked, pointing to a small photo that was pinned beside a woman's name in Michigan.

"Some of the women had photos of the bath bombs in question," Joan said. Monica just raised her eyebrows, surprised. "They said they often take photos of packages they receive so they can remember who sent it in case they want to message them or post and include their handle," Joan explained.

"Smart," was all Monica could think to say. She studied each of the photos on the board. Most were of opened boxes on kitchen countertops or in entry ways, but a few showed other opened packages nearby or clearly were in a nursery with baby things nearby.

"This is a beautiful baby quilt," Monica commented on of one of the photos. Joan looked. The quilt was familiar. "Yes, that's Rosie's photo. I've seen that quilt in her nursery. I'll ask her where she got it, it is really pretty. Very unique," Joan said. And then a memory flashed into her mind. She grabbed her laptop from the coffee table and opened her email.

"What?" Monica asked. Clearly alarmed from Joan's sudden urgency.

"Leena mentioned a baby blanket too. I don't know, something about the way she described it on the group call the first time I met her. It stands out. I'm emailing her to see if she has a photo of it," Joan said. She didn't know why a baby quilt would matter, it had been the bath bombs that seemed to connect it all. But she could feel goosebumps on her forearms, it was the feeling you have before a jump scare in a movie. She knew this was important, she just didn't know why.

CHAPTER 21

Pam
@freshlystitched

---

154 POSTS | **32.1K** FOLLOWERS | **2,597** FOLLOWING

It was just past noon when Pam heard a knock at her door. Caleb walked in, holding a brown box.

"Special delivery," he said, handing it to her. She looked at the box, confused. "Sorry, that was weird. It was just on your porch so I brought it in," he said. Pam laughed and she hoped he didn't realize she had thought it might be a present from him. Not that she expected anything. Caleb ran his hand through his hair, maybe he did realize.

"I hope tuna melts are OK for lunch? I honestly need to go grocery shopping," she said as she led the way back toward her kitchen. She had already started making the sandwiches.

"Sounds great. I really wasn't expecting anything when I texted this morning. I was just saying hi. But when you mentioned lunch and how close of a walk it is from work, I thought why not? You were right, it was a pretty walk," he said as he pulled himself up on her counter, sitting out of the way as she worked. Pam honestly hadn't expected him to take her up on her offer. He was working today and she was off, but she wanted to see him as soon as his name popped up on her screen. She was definitely falling for him, and it kind of scared her.

Caleb sat on the counter, right next to the package he had brought in from her porch. She saw him glance at it, so she walked over to see what it was. Maybe it was something embarrassing like a customer return? She didn't recognize the sender.

"Maybe I'm the only one, but I never get mail," he said with a laugh.

"I rarely do either. I'm kind of afraid to open it in front of you. But I have no idea why," she admitted.

"Well now you have to open it. Otherwise I'll assume the worst. I mean, what else can I do?"

Pam laughed as she ripped open the package. It was a few miscellaneous items, including some really nice fabric scissors with fancy copper handles. Caleb must have seen her confused face.

"Who's it from? Wait! Is it your birthday or something?" he seemed genuinely concerned he had missed her birthday.

"No, it's not. Honestly I don't know who this is from. Maybe a past customer? I have no idea. These scissors are really nice though. The rest of the stuff is pretty random."

"It's probably a fan since you're internet famous."

"Ha ha. No, I'm not. I know 32,000 followers might seem like a lot but I promise it's actually not that big. Most people who do that for living have over a hundred at least," she explained. Pam started to smell something burning. And she quickly moved back to the stove to flip the tuna melts.

"Shit. Well, one side is going to be a little burnt. Sorry," she said.

"I like it toasty," Caleb said and smiled this adorably cheesy smile. Pam almost couldn't stand it.

They ate in her plant room, since they'd texted that morning about her showing him her house plants, even though they both knew it was just an excuse to see each other again. And for a day date it wasn't going so bad. Without alcohol Pam always felt a little more awkward and unsure of herself.

"So, maybe this is heavy but I was curious," Caleb started. He looked unsure for a second but then continued. "The first time we hung out you mentioned you didn't want kids. Can you tell me more about that?"

"Why, do you want kids?" Pam asked.

"I don't know. Honestly I haven't thought too much about it either way. I guess that's why it stuck out to me that you sounded so sure on it. Like you have thought about it," he explained.

"I don't think men think about it as much. I mean, how often do you get asked?"

"If I want kids? Other than just now, I can't really think of a time."

"Yeah. It's different for women," she said. Caleb didn't respond; he just waited to see if she would elaborate.

"No, I don't want kids. If I'm being honest I don't know if anyone should really have kids. I mean, who even knows if our plant will be able to sustain life in future generations."

Caleb gave a few small nods, more like he was thinking on this not necessarily agreeing.

"So, you're worried about the environment. I get that," he said as he looked around at all her plants, taking them in. He spotted her gold coin cutting in a big jar by an open window. The breeze rustled its leaves slightly, it had grown a lot since he'd seen her cut it.

"Yes. But it's not just the environment. I mean, if you added up all the pain from longing for kids, losing kids, kids with problems parents didn't want to face, people who hurt kids including bad parents, the pain of living a life you didn't want but your parents forced on you by having you, I think the sum would be huge."

"But what about all the joy children feel for their parents and their lives generally, all the joy and love parents feel for their kids. I would think it probably would outweigh the pain sum. Don't you?"

"Source needed," Pam said as she rolled her eyes.

"What?" Caleb asked, confused. He seemed surprised by her tone.

"Cite your source," she clarified.

"Well, I can't. But you didn't cite a source either. We were just guessing at sums of pain vs joy. I don't know if you could actually measure that."

Pam felt dismissed. So, she got up and cleared their plates, taking them to the kitchen. She thought Caleb would follow her. Surely it was about time he walked back to work. She felt certain he probably wanted to. When she turned and saw he hadn't followed her, she went back to the plant room, where he was still seated.

"Did I do something wrong? I just wanted to talk. I'm not trying to upset you," he said.

"I'm getting the feeling you think I should want to have kids. Just like you think I should raise my prices on my shop items. I guess I'm feeling a little dismissed and I don't want to be in a relationship like that," said said, surprising even herself.

"Is this about your ex? Because I'm not him, Pam."

"No. It's not. Were either of the things I just listed about him? No. They were things you said."

"I never said you should want to have kids," Caleb shot back.

"I don't really want to do this. Let's just table it," Pam said and walked back toward the kitchen.

As Caleb started to rise to follow her a giant bird flew through Pam's window and landed in a water jug near the Gold Coin. The water was a rusty red color from the plant's seeds which had clearly fallen into the jug. At first the size of the bird had startled him, but now he saw it was just a common robin who was clearly very pregnant. The bird splashed and drank from the water, cooling itself. As it flapped its wings to fly away it jerked and sort of stumbled in the air. Caleb watched as it fell to the tiled floor, sputtering as if it had been struck. He wanted to reach out and help it but he didn't know if touching it was a good thing. He thought he'd heard before you shouldn't touch baby birds? Maybe adult birds were the same?

The robin convulsed on the ground as Caleb felt helpless and watched. It looked like the bird was injured, there was a little blood near its legs. But then he saw what looked like small, gooey eggs. They were mostly clear. It was immediately obvious to him the eggs were not viable. He saw the bird rise up and gently fly to the branch of the Gold Coin. She then flew off, leaving the mess behind.

He went into the kitchen to find paper towels or something to clean it up with.

"Just leave it. I'll clean it. You should get back to work," was all Pam said as she quickly led him out the door.

CHAPTER 22

Lacey
@laaacey

372 POSTS | **228** FOLLOWERS | **428** FOLLOWING

Lacey bent down and picked up two packages that were sitting by their front door before she entered the house. Her dog, Peanut, hopped up from his dog bed in the corner when he saw her come in. She doubted the ancient pug moved from the spot all day, but when she arrived home he moved quickly, knowing she'd give him a treat before letting him out the back door.

They'd bought this house just before they got married, almost three years ago now. She'd lovingly thrown herself into decorating that first year. Although she'd avoided the spare bedroom, as they'd hoped to get pregnant sooner than they did. It felt like a waste to decorate a room that could be turned into a nursery any day, although it had taken years. But now that she was well into her second trimester, it felt like the waiting and uncertainty was behind her. She wasn't sure who was more thrilled, her or her husband. She wouldn't be surprised if he came home with another little gift, either for her (compression socks—romance!) or for the baby. It was a lot, but she was so grateful for him. Their relationship had started off a bit strange after all, but they'd gotten through it together and soon they'd become parents together.

Peanut had done his business and was whining at the door to come back inside. The short jaunt around their tiny backyard was enough for him, she guessed. She let him back inside and moved to the kitchen to refresh his water bowl and set out his dinner. She'd almost forgotten the packages on the counter already. Pregnancy brain was real.

The first package was a book she'd ordered, *Bringing Up Bebe*. One of her mom friends swore by it, so she thought she'd give it a read. The second package was a small box, and she didn't recognize the return address. She used the kitchen scissors to cut open the tape. Inside was yellow tissue paper and a number of small containers. There was lip scrub, belly oil, room spray, and bath bombs. It was a little care package someone had made, how sweet. Although Lacey felt confused when she read the card:

> *Wishing you both the very best. Congrats on the new addition to your family.*
> *Sincerely,*
> *Pam*

She didn't know any Pams, did she? Maybe someone new at the office, or maybe it was someone James knew. Then it clicked! It was James' ex-wife. Lacey set the card back on top of the package and eyed the box suspiciously. James didn't talk about his ex often, but Lacey knew they had not stayed close. At all. So this was an odd and unexpected gift. She was sure Pam meant well, but it felt kind of off too. She left it on the counter and started making dinner, as she was starving, and James would be home soon.

"What's this?" he asked when he arrived home not 20 minutes later. Lacey was still finishing up dinner, which was baked chicken and pesto pasta. Last month she wouldn't have been able to handle the smell of this, but it was weird how quickly things changed and now she wanted to eat anything and everything all the time.

"She sent a gift, I guess kind of a baby congrats, although everything seems to be for me," Lacey answered.

"I see she's still going by Pam," he said as he read over the card.

"Is her middle name Ela? I've forgotten."

"No. Her name is Pamela. I just always called her Ela. That's what she was going by when we met. Sometime after the divorce she started going by Pam instead," James said. He looked confused, almost worried. "How does she know we're expecting? We don't talk. It kind of creeps me out that she knows."

"Oh, don't be silly. She probably saw on Facebook. I posted about it, remember. I told you. I wanted to make sure my extended family knew but I didn't want to call everyone."

"Are you friends on Facebook?" James asked.

"I don't know. I don't think so but maybe. I posted on Instagram too. Maybe she saw on there? It doesn't seem creepy to me that she would find out, Columbia is a small town anyway. It is kind of weird she sent a gift. But, I don't know, maybe she's burying the hatchet in a way or something?" Lacey guessed. The pasta was done, so she strained the water and tossed everything in butter and pesto. She placed the cooked chicken on two plates and doled out pasta between the two as well. Hers had the larger portion.

"Dinner's ready. Let's eat, I'm starving," Lacey said as she carried the plates toward the living room.

"Sounds good. Hey, do you want any of this stuff? It looks really homemade," he said, pulling a face.

"Not really. It was the thought that counts. You can toss it," she called as she placed the plates on the coffee table and grabbed the remote to their TV. James slid the entire box into the trash bin that was just under the counter. It nearly spilled out the top. He noted he should take the trash out after he ate dinner. He didn't want Lacey doing any work unless she had to. He just didn't want anything to happen to her, or their baby.

Pam paced around her house. She normally didn't include a return address on her packages, but she had to in order to get tracking and she wanted to know when this one arrived. It had been reckless, stupid really. But something inside her boiled over when she saw James' new wife post about being pregnant. Something inside her snapped and she had been less careful. She walked back and forth on the vintage rug in her sewing studio, ping ponging between her worktable and the crib that still sat in the room. Over the years she had convinced herself she was doing a service—to the women and to the world—with her packages. She was setting others free, and she was saving unborn babies from a horrible and painful life. Not to mention the population counter on her phone, ticking ever and ever higher. She was helping.

But this time, sending a package to Laaacey (she always said her name like this in her head because she clicked over to her Instagram profile more often than she wanted to admit) had been different. It had felt like revenge. Maybe she did have a Medea complex after all. But she didn't regret it. She was scared she might get caught though. Normally she never, ever included any identifying things on or in the packages. She even drove over state lines to mail them most of the time, so the postmarks couldn't all be traced back to Columbia, to her. But she'd even included a card this time—why?! It had been completely reckless no matter how good it had felt in the moment.

Due to the tracking, she knew the package had arrived this afternoon. She wondered if they'd gotten it. Maybe they were out of town, on a babymoon or whatever. Maybe she could get the package back without them knowing. She decided she had to try.

Pam got in her car and drove the ten minutes it took to get across town, to where she knew they lived. She hated the fact that the year after they had married she'd driven by every few weeks or so. No real reason, just to torture herself, she guessed. One time she thought Laaacey saw her, so she stopped. But now the route felt familiar. She switched on her headlights as the sun was setting, the evening taking over the sky. Perfect, if the package was on their porch she could more easily grab it without anyone seeing her.

She turned onto their street and spotted James. He was wheeling the trash bin to the curb. She nearly braked but realized that would only draw more attention to her. She kept the same speed and drove right past, and he didn't give her car so much as a look thankfully. So they were home. She was out of luck. Fuck. Their street ended in a cul-de-sac, so Pam rounded it slowly and began to drive back the way she came. James had already gone back inside. Pam could see their trash bin was very full, and the lid wouldn't even shut. Peeking out from the bin she could see a half-open trash bag. And she thought she could see the yellow tissue paper of her package peeking out! She parked a couple houses down and strolled past, trying to look like a neighbor on a walk. It was her package. She could see the entire contents still in the box, even the card sitting on top. The bath bombs were cracked and crumbling, the inky red seeds inside spilling out. She quickly got back in her car and drove home.

Pam should have felt relief. She wasn't caught, and they hadn't used the bath bombs. All that had come of her mistake was her ex getting a weird gift from her, which they had immediately thrown away. It should have been relief she felt. But as she poured red wine into her glass jar, she didn't feel anything like relief. She felt rage. How could they throw her gift away? So soon, and without using anything? The card was even sitting on top. It wasn't like she'd expected a thank you card, but that seemed really cold. Was she really so insignificant to them that a handmade gift was nothing but trash in their eyes?

She sat on her kitchen floor with her wine, drinking and scrolling. Trying to calm herself down. It wasn't working. And then she saw a post that fanned the flames she had inside already. It was @ bedofrosies. She was apparently still pregnant and was sharing some maternity portraits she'd gotten. Tagging the photographer, who probably did them for her for free. She'd never sent someone a package twice. Too reckless. Pam refilled her glass and headed to her studio room. She still had a couple bath bombs from the last batch she'd made for Laaacey. She looked up Rosie's address again; she'd saved them all. And she packaged up another box, adding other random gifts including things that were heavily branded, so it might seem like a gift from a sponsor. She taped the box up and added the address. It didn't have far to go. Maybe she'd get her this time.

Now Pam felt the rage subside. She looked at the tidy box and felt powerful. She felt purpose. She wasn't insignificant. She was changing the world.

CHAPTER 23

Abby
@alwaysabby

5,099 POSTS	**478K** FOLLOWERS	**1,349** FOLLOWING

Abby couldn't really say what had compelled her to get involved. As if she didn't have enough on her plate already. But something in her craved something beyond work and momming. She loved her career and she loved her son, of course, but there were times where she felt less than human. She probably should have just gotten a hobby, make candles or something. But sometimes it all felt like it would end up bleeding into her influencer work, so then it was just career stuff again. She wanted to spend some of her time on something she just wanted to do, not because she had to do it but because it interested her. It felt like a little rebellion. Although if it was then it was the lamest rebellion in the world.

And that's how Abby found herself reading through email after email once her son was tucked in bed and the dishes were put away. Joan had been vague but had filled them in on some details of where her story was taking her since she had met them at RTLAS. She mentioned having far too many emails she could follow up on, and something in Abby filed it away. She contacted Joan and asked if she could help. She said she could answer emails, and she also knew how to keep her mouth shut. Surprisingly, Joan had taken her up on it immediately.

She logged into the email box Joan had set up. There were well over 100 emails, which didn't scare Abby one bit. The three groupings Joan had created didn't go deep enough for Abby, so she had added subgroups. Joan had told her the bare bones of what she was looking for, but she had also kept some details vague. Abby got the sense Joan didn't want her to become biased as she worked, and she also could tell Joan wasn't entirely sure what she was looking for either. When Rosie had asked her why Joan wanted a picture of her baby quilt, Abby had truthfully answered that she didn't know, but even if she had known she wouldn't have said.

Tonight, she was writing back to the emails in group three, which she called the 'my friend may know something' group. The main goal for this group was to read every single email, because you never know, and to write back just so they knew the email had been received and that someone on the other side cared enough to write back. Given the emails were all about miscarriages, Joan felt it was important that every email get some response, even a short one. Abby agreed. It just felt decent, even if the digital world wasn't always filled with decency.

She was eating a small bowl of mint chocolate chip ice cream, which she hid in the back of the freezer and only ate when her son was in bed. It was her secret. See? She could keep secrets. She nearly dropped the spoon from her mouth when she read the next email:

Joan,
I saw your posting on the message board and I wanted to get in touch. It's about my friend, Avery. She died last year, and her death was really tragic and strange. She was pregnant at

the time, and it was still early but I don't know how far along she was. Her husband was out of town, so I was staying over this one weekend. I did that sometimes when her husband was gone. They lived in this big old house that was gorgeous but definitely felt haunted. She hated sleeping there alone. Anyway, it was a normal night. We ordered pizza and watched a movie, some old romantic comedy like The Wedding Planner or something. I don't remember. Then we headed off to bed, and Avery said her back was hurting so she was going to soak for a while.

I guess I should say, the room I would stay in was on the second floor. Their bedroom was on the first floor. The house had kind of a weird layout. Like I said, it was old. I went to bed but woke up in the night with a headache. I went down to the kitchen to get some Advil when I saw the light on under her bedroom door, which seemed weird as I knew she liked to sleep in complete darkness and with a sound machine (we've traveled together). I kind of wondered if she'd fallen asleep in the tub, she'd been really exhausted lately. And of course, this worried me, so after knocking and not hearing anything I went in.

She was in the tub, but she wasn't asleep — she was dead. She looked almost blue. It was horrible. The water was ice cold and I thought she'd been stabbed or something because the water was this dark red color. But I pulled her out of the tub and it wasn't blood, it was a bath bomb she'd used. The whole thing felt like a horror movie.

I know they did an autopsy since her death was so sudden. And I remember she didn't drown, which was what I thought

at first. Her husband would have all the details, it was hon-
estly too much for me at the time.

She was waiting to find out the sex, but she had the
names picked out. If it had been a girl she wanted to name her
Allison. If it was a boy, Jeffery. I don't know why I'm telling
you this part, but I think about those names all the time. Av-
ery was the kindest, most hilarious woman I've ever known. I
miss her every day.

If you were going to include something about her, I'd
want you to get permission from her husband too. We still get
lunch from time to time but we haven't in some months. I
doubt he will ever completely heal. I know I won't.
Yours Truly,
Erin

Abby felt a tear slide down her cheek. She wrote Erin back, trying to comfort her. She shared her personal email and IG handle in case she wanted to connect. And she saved the email to show Joan. Although the story was second hand, it did mention bath bombs specifically. It felt important. She wondered what Joan would make of it, if she would try to reach out to the husband.

CHAPTER 24

Joan
@thisisnow_podcast

613 POSTS | **54.7K** FOLLOWERS | **56** FOLLOWING

J oan sat in the waiting room, trying not to touch anything. The room felt like an expensive spa and not at all like a doctor's office. She didn't even want to think about what this whole process could cost. Across from her two men sat, holding hands. They smiled at her, Joan smiled back so as not to look rude. She rose when Monica walked into the room.

"Hey, sorry I'm late. What's wrong, you look worried?" Monica said.

"No, I'm fine. I'm glad we're doing this. You were right. There's nothing wrong with getting all the information. It doesn't mean we're committed, just learning more. I'm good," Joan said. She was apprehensive still about having a child, but she did think Monica was right, it doesn't hurt to research.

"What is it then? You look a little pale," Monica probed. Joan sighed.

"It's work. Which I realize I've been a little obsessed with lately," Joan started. Monica nodded her agreement but wanted her to go on. She did. "I heard back from Jackie about the other woman's pathology report. I need to call her as her email was too medical for me to fully understand, but the gist of it was that this second woman's report was very similar to Jackie's. So, either both their babies have the same rare genetic condition or they were both exposed to the same substance," Joan said. Monica took this in for a moment.

"So, it's possible they were both poisoned?"

"Yes. It's possible. In fact, it seems likely," Joan said.

"And they both took baths using bath bombs on the days they miscarried?"

"Yes."

"And you know Jackie's bath bomb came from Rosie. Does the other woman remember where she got hers?" Monica asked. Joan took a deep breath before she answered.

"She said she also got it in the mail, a gift from a follower she assumed. Just like Leena."

"That's it then, right? That's the connection. These anonymous bath bombs are inducing miscarriages. Now you just have to figure out who's sending them."

"That's what I'm worried about: I have no idea how," Joan said, hanging her head. Monica had never seen Joan get so absorbed in her work. Sure, she worked hard and loved her job, and she was a naturally curious person. But this felt different. It was starting to feel personal. Monica worried what would happen if Joan couldn't get to the bottom of this.

She saw Joan's phone light up, Rosie's name flashing onto the screen. Joan tapped to send the call to voicemail.

"I'll call her after. Surely we're about to go in," Joan said. Just then the nurse called Monica's name, as she had made the appointment. Joan's phone buzzed again. A text from Rosie. They could only see the first part of the message that read:

I got bath bombs in the mail...

Joan and Monica did a double take.

"Call her. I'll reschedule this," Monica said. She rose to talk to the nurse. Joan did as she was told.

"Joan, I'm sorry but I just opened it. I called right away," Rosie said as soon as she answered Joan's call. She was clearly freaking out. "I don't understand all the connections you've made, but I know it's all got something to do with bath bombs. I was opening my packages from today, and I nearly dropped the box once I saw what was inside. Should I throw it away?"

"No, don't throw it away. In fact, as much as you can don't touch it," Joan said. She didn't want to freak Rosie out more, but this could be it. This could be how she can find out where these are coming from.

"Could we FaceTime? I want to see the package, if that's OK?" Joan asked.

"Sure. I'll call you back." Rosie hung up and called Joan back via FaceTime. She flipped the camera and showed Joan the box. There were two bath bombs wrapped in plastic bags. They were a kind of rusty red color, like the desert floor. There were a few other items in the box, but everything seemed random and boldly branded. The bath bombs were the only items that didn't seem to indicate any kind of company name, like they could have come from anywhere. Joan asked to see the outside of the box, which Rosie did. There was no return address. But the post mark indicated a 65802 zip code. Rosie said she knew it, it was from Springfield, which was only about three hours away from Kansas City.

"What should I do with this? Should I take it to the police or something?" Rosie asked. Joan thought.

"Even if I shared everything I have with the police, I don't know if it would make a difference yet or not. I just don't know if there's enough for them to go on," Joan explained. But then she had an idea.

"Take it to Jackie. See if she can run lab tests on them," Joan said.

"Jackie? Wait, what would she be testing for?" Rosie asked. Joan knew she probably needed to fully explain her theory now. She was as sure as she could likely be. Rosie listened and got very quiet.

"Are you still there?" Joan asked. She was scared that maybe they had been disconnected.

"Still here," Rosie said in a small voice. Joan gave her a minute. When she started to talk again she could hear the quiver in her voice. "The bath bombs I gave Jackie might have been poisoned. So, I helped kill Jackie's baby?"

"No," Joan said firmly. "It's still just a theory for one thing. And even if I'm right, you didn't know, Rosie. How could you have known?" Joan tried to reassure her, but she could still hear Rosie softly crying on the other end. Joan let her. She just listened and waited for her to speak. She and Monica had gone down the elevator but were still in the lobby. Monica was listening, and she rubbed Joan's arm.

"OK. I'll take them to Jackie. I'll see if she can test them for poison. If they can't at the hospital I bet she'll know where to take them," Rosie sounded sad but determined. Joan told her again it wasn't her fault before they hung up. After she did, Joan surprised herself and started to cry. Monica hugged her and said, "I think you should go to Kansas City." Joan just nodded.

CHAPTER 25

Rosie
@bedofrosies

| **2,576** POSTS | **239K** FOLLOWERS | **788** FOLLOWING |

osie tried to breathe as she drove to the airport to pick up Joan. She was now 36 weeks pregnant and her basketball of a belly felt like it barely fit behind the wheel. She often felt like she was gasping for breath when she sat in certain positions and her car seat did her no favors.

She had been unable to sleep the night before, which was not all that unusual these days as she seemed to spend half the night getting up to pee and the other half wrestling with her pregnancy pillow trying to get comfortable enough to sleep. Now that her bump was more like a mountain, she noticed she got a lot more unsolicited advice. And if she heard one more person say, "Sleep now, while you still can." She was going to scream at them: HOW?!

But last night she'd been unable to sleep for an entirely different reason. She was at least partly the reason Jackie had miscarried. And the weight of this fact clung to her. It felt like a stain she couldn't wash off. She understood she hadn't known, she hadn't intended. But the fact was, she had contributed. Plus, who was this person sending her bath bombs trying to kill her baby? Clearly, they knew they hadn't succeeded the first time, so they had sent her more. What the fuck was wrong with the world? She had to do whatever she could to help Joan track this psycho down. If nothing else, she had to do it for Jackie.

She slammed on her brakes as she almost drove past Joan's gate, lost in her thoughts. She spotted her, squinting into the early afternoon sunlight. Joan was even taller than Rosie had expected. She tossed her bag in the backseat before opening the passenger door of the car.

"Forgot my sunglasses. I always forget something," Joan said with a smile.

"Here, I have some random pairs in here," Rosie said, flipping up the center console of her car as she pulled away from the curb. "Take your pick. They're yours for the trip."

"How are you holding up?" Joan asked. She could sense the low-level anxiety filling the car. She was probably contributing to some of it herself.

"Oh, you know. I'm about to become a mom any day now and someone out there wants to kill my baby, and I may have helped them kill my friend's baby," Rosie said. She took one hand off the wheel to swipe at her left eye. Joan kept facing forward but gently placed her hand on Rosie's shoulder.

"It's not your fault. I'm sure Jackie told you the same."

"Of course, she did. But it doesn't make it hurt less," Rosie paused to collect herself a little. She took another deep breath. She couldn't go into labor right now.

"She said we could meet her at the hospital at the end of her shift today, at 6:00. She said she should have the toxicology report by then," Rosie said.

"Wow, that seems fast. I swear anytime I've gotten a test done by my doctor I had to wait at least two weeks to get the results," Joan said, trying to lighten the mood. It didn't work.

Twenty minutes later they pulled into Rosie's driveway. The house was white with a pink front door. Joan noticed the door mat that said, "Live, Laugh, Love." Rosie saw where her eyes had darted and immediately blurted out, "It's from RTLAS white elephant gift swap. Carmen bought it for me." And Joan thought she saw just the hint of a smile tug at Rosie's mouth.

"You know, you don't have to put it out just because she gave it to you," Joan said.

"I know. But my husband hates it so much I couldn't help myself," Rosie admitted. That made Joan laugh, which she realized she needed.

Joan followed Rosie into her house, which was clean and tidy and smelled like lavender. She offered to make coffee, but Joan said she wanted to take a power nap before their meeting later. Rosie said she might just do the same. She led Joan toward the guest room, walking past the nursery as they went. She saw Joan peeking in.

"It's all set up, finally. I wanted everything done before the arrival of our little gal. I hope she loves it."

"I'm sure she will," Joan said. She had taken a few steps into the room. She noticed the baby quilt draped over the side of the crib. She didn't even realize she'd walked over to it until she was touching it. She'd seen it in the photo Rosie had texted her. It looked a lot like Leena's, who she had also asked to text her a picture. Leena had seemed as confused by it as Rosie, but she'd done it. Rosie noticed Joan touching the quilt.

"You know, I was thinking about it after you asked me for that picture. I can't be 100% sure but I think that quilt arrived the same day I got the first package of bath bombs. I think. At least I vaguely remember it being around as I gathered up other things to take to Jackie." At the mention of this, Joan could see Rosie's brow furrow.

"Do you know who sent it?"

"Yes. Hang on, let me look it up," Rosie said, pulling out her phone. "I know I posted about it on my blog," she explained as she scrolled. "That's why most people send things. They are hoping you post about it and it's marketing for them. I don't normally accept many gifts because of that, it's hard to keep track of everything. But when this gal messaged me her quilts were so beautiful I said yes. Oh, here it is," Rosie turned her phone's screen toward Joan. She'd already clicked over to an Instagram account that seemed like it was for an Etsy shop. Joan pulled out her phone and searched the name. She found the account and took a screenshot, not wanting to follow it yet as sometimes people noticed that kind of thing.

Rosie showed Joan to the guest room and left her, so they could both grab a nap. Joan had been tired, her flight being so early this morning but now she felt restless. She wanted to know what Jackie had found. What if the bath bombs came back as just that, harmless bath bombs? What then? It wasn't like it was such an unusual gift to give someone. And why was she so obsessed with these baby quilts?

She wasn't falling asleep, so she pulled out her phone and navigated to the quilt shop account again. She scrolled through the posts, each one showed off an item from the seller's shop and said something about it. Not the most riveting content, but her items were very pretty. Then Joan scrolled to one that made her stop. It was Leena's quilt, she was sure of it. All the caption said was, "Sending off another round of baby quilts. More in the shop next week!" So the same person had sent Leena and Rosie a baby quilt after seeing them announce their pregnancies online. Joan tapped to see who the account was following, which was well over 2,000 other accounts. As she scrolled she saw lots of influencers she recognized, many of whom had emailed her recently with stories of miscarriages after using bath bombs. She bolted upright in the bed.

When Rosie came downstairs later, Joan was already sitting on a chair in the entryway. She was practically vibrating, and Rosie thought it was because she was ready to meet with Jackie.

"I know how she gets the addresses," Joan said.

"What!?" Rosie asked

"Or, I should say, I have a theory."

"Tell me in the car. I don't want to be late," Rosie said, grabbing her purse, realizing now she'd slept longer than she'd meant to. The two headed toward the hospital, Rosie breathing heavily behind the wheel again.

"Are you sure you don't want me to drive? I know I'm a former New Yorker, but I swear I can drive," Joan offered.

"No, no, really I'm fine. So, how does this person get our addresses?"

"It's the baby quilts. She sees you announce on Instagram. She sends a message asking to send you a quilt. Or maybe she's already sent you something in the past, I guess that could be the case too? Anyway, when you say yes, she gets your address. She sends the quilt. And that's the end of the story as far as you're concerned. But now she has your address, so she could, if she wanted, send a second package."

Rosie seemed skeptical. She didn't say anything for a few moments.

"But, anyone could do it," she finally said.

"What do you mean?"

"I mean, and I know how this is going to sound but, I get gifts from followers all the time. People want to send things a lot, like I said it's mostly because they want you to post about it, so they get more sales. I've given my mailing address out to at least 20 people I don't know just this year," Rosie said.

"You're right. And I'm not saying it's for sure this woman. I could totally be wrong. This is a working theory based on the fact both you and Leena were sent quilts by this person and you both also got bath bomb packages."

"OK. So, it could be this person. And it could totally be someone else. But what else do we know about this person other than she sews and has an Etsy? Because again, that's probably thousands of people."

"I tried to look her up some while I couldn't nap. Her Etsy shop says she's based in Columbia, Missouri. That's pretty close to here, right?"

"Yes, like a couple hours south."

"Her name is Pamela and her shop name is Freshly Stitched. From what I could tell it looked like she used to have a personal Instagram account called @justanotherela. I saw one commenter reference it on a very old post, and then I looked at the @justanotherela account and it doesn't have much on it but one of the last posts says to follow her new shop and it tags Freshly Stitched. And, like I said there aren't a lot of posts on the Ela account but there was a very old photo of the front of her house. It's a yellow bungalow and the house next door is navy blue."

"Okay," Rosie said. Still clearly skeptical.

"She's following a lot of the women who have contacted me and also had bath bomb miscarriages," at this fact Rosie's eyebrows rose, "and it seems like she really likes plants," Joan concluded as they pulled in the hospital parking lot.

"Everyone likes plants," Rosie said while parking.

"Maybe I should say, it seems like she works with plants. She mentioned something in a caption about getting back to her 'work plants.' So, I'm guessing she's a florist or owns a greenhouse or something."

"Why does that matter?"

Joan followed Rosie's lead as they headed into the towering building. They walked toward the elevators and entered as a family poured out. Once the doors closed, Joan continued.

"Because, if we are dealing with someone who uses poison then the next question is: where do they get the poison? Do they work at a pharmacy? Do they have access to narcotics? If she has access to poisonous plants or is experienced enough to grow her own, that might mean something," Joan explained.

"Feels like a stretch, but honestly this whole thing sounds like a weird nightmare and not real life." The two women watched as the numbers lit up, the elevator rising. The whole theory still hinged on the toxicology report from Jackie. Joan wondered what it would say.

CHAPTER 26

Jackie
@docjackie

| **106** POSTS | **328** FOLLOWERS | **452** FOLLOWING |

Jackie ushered the women into her office. Her nurse practitioner raised her eyebrows as Jackie shut her door. Not only did she rarely shut her office door, she also didn't often stay after hours. Or at least, she hadn't much this year. Joan and Rosie took the seats across from her desk. Jackie automatically offered Rosie an extra seat cushion for her back, which she took. With nearly all her patients being pregnant women, Jackie knew how uncomfortable those chairs, and probably all chairs, were at a certain point. She sat down behind her desk, and the meeting all of sudden felt serious and formal. She flipped open a file before she spoke.

"The sample the lab tested came back positive for cytisine, which is a toxin. It can interfere with breathing, although I don't think there are many cases where it caused death. I'm not a poison expert, so since getting the lab results I've been trying to do some research, but there's not much in the literature on cytisine. Apparently, there are some trials being done in New Zealand with a substance that includes cytisine for helping patients quit smoking. The drug in development is supposed to help with cravings and withdrawals from nicotine," Jacki paused, reading over her notes. "Honestly that's really about all I have so far. It does seem there is a toxic substance in at least this bath bomb you sent for testing, but it's not clear to me this could cause a miscarriage. We'd have to test that somehow in order to be sure,"

"What is the origin of cytisine? Like, is it made in a lab?" Joan asked.

"It's found in seeds. I think it's a type of tree. But again, not really my field so I'd want to research more."

Joan gave Rosie a knowing look. Rosie looked pale, then she began to cry. For a moment the women just sat together, taking in the news.

"That's what I have to share, is there more you wish to share with me?" Jackie asked.

Joan looked at Rosie, who gave a small shrug.

"Well, it depends. How involved do you want to be? I am starting to have a theory, but it's pretty loose at this point," Joan explained. For a moment Jackie almost looked troubled, almost angry.

"How involved do I want to be? I just had the lab test a bath bomb. They looked at me like I was crazy, until the results came back positive. This bath bomb was sent to my very pregnant friend, presumably to harm her unborn child. And it seems possible this is the reason I lost my pregnancy. I'd say I am about as involved as you can get."

"True. I'm sorry. I'm not used to dragging so many people along as I research. It feels almost wrong. Like, I should solve this and then get back to you. I don't know. This whole thing is just weird, and wrong, and like nothing I've ever reported on before," Joan said almost in a whisper by the end. As if saying it aloud made it all the more true. But it was already true, and probably bigger than she even realized.

"Joan thinks she has a lead. Maybe." Rosie blurted. She looked to Joan for confirmation and she nodded.

"Tell me everything. I want to know," Jackie said.

At some point the women had moved their meeting down to the cafeteria. Joan and Jackie sipped hot tea while Rosie drank hot chocolate and picked at a very old looking donut. Joan laid out her theory as best she could, with Rosie showing pictures of the quilt and Pamela's account on her phone. Jackie listened intently, not asking any questions until Joan was done. Joan had the sneaking suspicion that perhaps Jackie could see how wacky the theory was and was about to punch holes in it. Joan even wondered if this is what she hoped for. It's probably what Monica could do too if she were here.

"You seem to have a working theory of who and how. Pamela would have had the opportunity, as she clearly had both Rosie's and Leena's addresses and presumably had a way to get others too. You also suspect she works with plants, although no clear evidence of the particular plant in question yet," Jackie seemed to be talking more to herself. Laying things out. Thinking.

"But what about the why? What's her motivation to do this? If it's true, she's creating poisonous bath bombs and mailing them anonymously to pregnant women hoping to cause miscarriage; why? It seems very extreme."

"I don't know. I'm not really a crime reporter, even though I have covered a few. I know about as much about murders as anyone and this doesn't make much sense to me either. It's clearly not a crime of passion, she's planning these and she's careful about them. It's also pretty clear the target is unborn babies. I have no evidence for a motive yet. But given this is a larger plot, like she does this over and over, it could be some kind of manifesto type thinking. Like how the Unabomber thought he was fighting against the evils of the technological revolution and actually helping humans to become free. Perhaps this person, whoever they are, believes they are doing some kind of good with this act," Joan said.

"What's next? I guess you try to prove or disprove your theory?" Jackie asked. Joan hadn't totally thought about the next steps yet. The whole thing felt overwhelming.

"Ok, let's say you're right. Our girl Pamela is the bath bomb maker. Shouldn't we go to the police so this stops? What if she's going to mail another package tomorrow to someone? She's clearly still at it if she just mailed this to me," Rosie said, some panic rising in her.

"What are the police going to do with this? The most 'evidence' we have is the toxicology report and all it really says is yes there's a poisonous substance in a bath bomb we were mailed. That's it though, that's basically all we have," Jackie said. Joan noted her use of the word 'we' and couldn't help but feel a little relieved that she wasn't descending into madness on her own.

"But you're right Rosie, we have to move forward, because for all we know this person is mailing out more bath bombs tomorrow and they have to be stopped," Jackie said. Her eyes misting, which surprised all three women. Rosie reached across the table and grabbed her hand. Jackie squeezed back.

"Let's test the theory. I don't know how we could safely test the bath bomb, like if it can actually cause a miscarriage. But we probably could learn more about this woman, Pamela, and at least cross her off as a suspect or not," Joan said. She didn't add more, and it became clear she wasn't certain how to do this yet. The women sipped their drinks and thought.

"What if you interview her?" Rosie started, "Did you say you thought she might be located in Columbia? What if you ask if you can interview her in person. Try to find out if she has some kind of manifesto or whatever. And while you interview her, maybe I can have a look around her house or something."

"What? You can't break into her house?" Joan said.

"OK, then forget you heard that part. I'll just drive you to Columbia and you can interview her and I'll just wait in the car," Rosie said. Clearly lying.

"I'll go," Jackie said. Joan and Rosie stared at her. "If Rosie is going to, well, wait in the car while Joan interviews her, I can be the lookout for Rosie while she…does that."

"Guys, I know you're planning to break into her house. I don't think that's a good idea. It's a crime. What if you're caught?" Joan pointed out.

"We need to find enough evidence to get the police involved. Short of her confessing to you, we're not going to get it unless we find something more concrete. I mean, even if you interview her and she clearly has some motive, what does that really prove? Still nothing we can take to the police," Jackie said. Joan thought. She wanted to disagree. But she knew Jackie was right. They didn't have much unless they found something that showed Pamela was the bath bomb mailer. But if she wasn't, then wouldn't that mean they were just breaking into an innocent person's house? It wasn't a great plan, but she couldn't think of something better that could move them closer to finding the killer.

"She might not agree to meet with me," Joan pointed out.

"Message her. I bet she'll either write back right away, or not at all," Rosie said.

Before Joan could overthink it, she pulled out her phone and sent Pam's account a DM:

> Hi there. I'm working on a story for the podcast about influencer marketing. I'd love some perspectives from people who are on both sides of it. Could I interview you?

Once she hit 'send' she put her phone face down on the table. As if the device was very hot.

"Give it 30 minutes. I bet she writes back," Rosie said.

"Really? Who looks at their phone that often?" Jackie asked.

"Lots of us," Rosie said a little sheepishly.

"Let's make a list of questions I can ask her while we wait, otherwise I'm going to lose my mind," Joan suggested.

The women started coming up with fake interview questions, many of which were actually pretty good. Joan wrote them down in her little notebook, scribbling away. After some time, Jackie said she needed to head home, but to call her if they heard back from Pamela. She wanted to be kept in the loop and she insisted she was going with them to Columbia if it happened. They agreed.

As Joan and Rosie headed to the parking lot, Joan asked for Rosie's keys, which she finally surrendered. She climbed into the passenger side, adjusting the seat so she was almost laying on her back but at least she could breathe. She navigated Joan back toward her house.

"Do you mind if I check your messages?" Rosie asked, holding up Joan's phone. Joan said go ahead and told her the passcode. Rosie tapped to open the app and nearly dropped the phone on the floor board.

"She wrote back!"

"What did she say?"

> Hi Joan. Love the podcast. I'd be happy to be interviewed although I don't know if I'll have much to say. How do you like to do them, over the phone?'

Rosie read, her eyes wide. "I told you she'd write back!"

"OK. So I need to meet her in person. How should I position that? Can you type:"

> Great. Are you based in Missouri? I thought your Etsy shop said that somewhere. I'm in Kansas City on another story this week. Could we meet in person?

Rosie dutifully typed out the message and sent it. They nearly missed the last turn to Rosie's house, getting completely caught up in messaging Pam. Joan parked the car in front of the house, the headlights showed a box sitting on the doorstep. She looked to Rosie.

"I ordered a pizza before we left the hospital. I know this is all really dark but I'm still 36 weeks pregnant and I'm really hungry all the time," Rosie said by way of explanation. Joan laughed.

They sat around Rosie's kitchen island, eating pizza off of Rosie's monogrammed plates. Joan checked her messages again, she had a new one. She read it aloud:

> Yes, I am in Missouri but I'm in Columbia. It's about 2 hours away from KC. Can that fit your travel schedule?

Joan wrote back (and read it aloud as she did):

> I've learned over the years I am a better interviewer in person than I am on the phone. So a short drive is worth it to me. Would it be possible to meet sometime tomorrow or the following day? I'm flexible.

"You're being so casual. Honestly, you'd be a great secret agent," Rosie said. Joan laughed again. She was glad to see Rosie in a somewhat better mood, perhaps the pizza had revived her. Also, maybe having a game plan helped too.

"You know, I really don't like the idea of you or Jackie breaking into someone's house. I'm not sure this person is the mailer, what if she's not? Plus, it's dangerous. You could get caught, someone else could be home, who knows," Joan said. Rosie took her time finishing the big bite of pizza she'd just taken before she looked Joan in the eyes and spoke.

"If Pamela is not the mailer, then the worst thing is I will be inside her home. I'm not going to take anything or harm her life in any way," she could see Joan wanted to respond but she held up a finger and continued, "but if this Pamela IS the mailer then I know I won't regret doing this. If your theory is right, she tried to kill my baby. Twice. And it was her package that caused Jackie to miscarry. Not to mention Leena and all the women we may not even know about yet. I know it's sort of crazy, but it's worth the risk," Rosie said. "Plus, imagine you're a police officer and you find a 36-week pregnant woman has broken into someone's house. That'll be a first for them for sure, right? Maybe I can talk my way out of it," Rosie said with a wink. Joan heard in her voice the nervousness just beneath the joke, but she smiled back at Rosie all the same. Then she picked up her phone again. She had another message:

> Tomorrow afternoon works for me. There's a little coffee shop / wine bar near my house @showmecoffee Could we meet there around 4pm?

As Joan messaged her back to say yes, Rosie was already calling Jackie to tell her the news. They were headed to Columbia to test their theory.

CHAPTER 27

Rosie
@bedofrosies

| **2,578** POSTS | **240K** FOLLOWERS | **788** FOLLOWING |

Never had a morning gone by so quickly and so slowly at the same time Rosie thought as she and Joan pulled into Jackie's driveway to pick her up. She had fully given up driving, and Joan was behind the wheel. The women had decided to carpool down to Columbia for the interview, so they could talk and strategize on the way. Jackie walked out of her house carrying three thermal mugs and a Tupperware of cookies. Rosie spotted them immediately. She hadn't felt this kind of constant hunger since she had run track in high school; it was annoying really.

"I like that we're going to try and potentially catch a murderer and you brought baked goods," Joan said as Jackie climbed into the back seat.

"It's very Sherlock's mother of me, I know, but I couldn't sleep last night. So, I baked."

"I had a hard time sleeping too. I mean, I do every night now since I have to pee every 20 minutes but also, I was thinking about today. I can't decide if I want this Pamela person to be the mailer, or not. And I've never broken into a house before, so I was thinking about the logistics of that too I guess," Rosie said. She saw Joan's brow furrow as she drove.

"I think I should be the one to go into the house," Jackie said.

"What? No. I'm doing it."

"Rosie, you're extremely pregnant. I may not be your doctor but I'm still a doctor and I don't feel right letting you go in there. What if you went into labor, or got hurt?" Jackie pointed out.

"Jackie, I'm going in. For one, I gave you that bath bomb. I will never get over it, but this is something I can do. And also," she paused, clearly thinking, "look I'm just going to say it. I'm a white pregnant lady, you're black. Who do you think has a better chance if they do get caught breaking and entering?"

"Don't use my race against me. And don't lecture me about how race works in this country," Jackie said. Rosie felt herself wince. The car was silent for a few moments, then Jackie let out a sigh.

"And you don't have to hold yourself responsible for giving me the bath bomb. I don't, so you shouldn't either. It's not helping any of us for you to do that to yourself," Jackie said, a little softer.

"I'm sorry, but it's going to be me who goes into the house," Rosie said.

"Let's flip for it?"

"Fine. Heads I go, tails you go," Rosie said as Jackie fished a coin out of her purse. She flipped it in the back seat, caught it, and turned it over on the top of her hand. She held it forward, so she and Rosie saw the results at the same time. It was heads.

"For the record, I still don't think anyone should go into the house. I might learn a lot from the fake interview, who knows?" Joan said. But she could tell Rosie and Jackie had made up their minds.

Pam scrolled through the message board, reading what was new from yesterday. It wasn't much. She and Caleb were on a break, or maybe broken up, she wasn't sure. So she'd been spending more time catching up with her friends who frequented the antinatalism board as she'd kind of neglected them while she'd been dating him. How cliché. She guessed she wasn't immune to being kind of a basic bitch herself.

She closed her laptop and headed to her bathroom. She needed to put on a little makeup before she left for the interview. She hated to admit it, but she was really excited. She'd heard Joan's podcast many times. And it was really cool to be recognized for her work as a handmade artist. Plus, the more she thought about it, the more she realized she actually did have a lot to say about influencer marketing and selling online. Pam wasn't exactly an expert, but she was really immersed in that world. So it was cool to get to talk to someone she admired about something she knew a lot about. Now she just needed to address the bags under her eyes. She stared at herself in the mirror. She looked tired.

Pam pushed the plastic drugstore bag off the vanity and pulled out her makeup bag. She'd almost forgotten about her late night run the evening before. She'd been feeling really sick, but wasn't sure if she needed Tums or maybe had a little touch of food poisoning or what. While she was in the store, walking down the aisles shopping for a cure it dawned on her that it felt eerily similar to a sickness she'd had once before, years ago. On a whim she decided to buy a pregnancy test, just so she could rule it out. The store had them in a glass case. She had to get an employee who was clearly at least 15 years younger than her to open the case. A small humiliation on its own. She felt better by the time she'd gotten home, so she forgot about it all and had gone to bed. The whole idea was comical now, in the light of day.

Pam tapped her phone's screen, mostly out of habit. She saw she was late to meet Joan. Shit. She quickly swiped some concealer on and dusted some blush on her pale cheeks. Then she tugged a beanie over her messy hair as she exited her little yellow bungalow's front door. She'd have to walk quickly so she wasn't a rude amount of late.

Jackie and Rosie watched as Pamela left her house and started walking briskly toward the coffee shop they had dropped Joan at nearly an hour before. They had driven around before, finding her house based on the front door photo she had posted online. Once they found it, they dropped Joan and parked near the house but far enough away they felt they wouldn't be seen. Luckily the neighborhood had lots of cars parked on the street, it wasn't exactly busy, but it certainly wasn't deserted. Rosie felt this was good for hiding their car, but she wasn't sure how she was going to break into the house without anyone seeing. They both watched as Pam emerged from the house, turned a corner toward the coffee shop, and was then out of sight.

"As soon as you get into the house, call me. I want to be on the phone the whole time, so if she returns I can tell you," Jackie said. Rosie nodded. She could feel her hands shaking a little. She exited the car and walked as casually as she could toward the house. She quickly checked to see if anyone was walking by, or any neighbors were watching. When she didn't see anyone, she opened the gate to the backyard. She had brought a few crackers, in case there was a dog but luckily there wasn't. She quickly walked through the backyard toward the back door. She figured she'd try this first since climbing in through a window with her belly was pretty much out of the question. To her great surprise, and she also realized dread, the back door was open. She walked in, shut it, and called Jackie who picked up immediately.

"I'm in. The door was unlocked," Rosie said. She was wearing winter gloves, the kind with the special fingertips that allow you to still use your phone. She felt like an idiot. She felt exposed. What was she doing in a stranger's house?! She took a deep breath.

"I hear your breathing Rosie. Are you OK? I can come in there, we can switch," Jackie said.

"No, I'm good. Just nervous. So far, no alarms. I guess someone who leaves their back door unlocked isn't too concerned about break-ins."

"Just tell me everything you see. You can do this. And let's keep moving in case the interview is short. Joan can't control everything."

Rosie took a moment to look around. It was beautiful. She realized she'd seen the room before. "I'm in a sunroom and it's full of plants. Like, it feels like a greenhouse," she began to narrate as she walked through the house. She tried to quickly get a sense of the layout, where the living spaces were, the bedrooms, the bathroom, the exits. She narrated anything and everything to Jackie who mostly listened with a few "Yes"s or "OK"s as she made her way around the house. She tried not to touch anything she didn't have to. She really wanted to use the bathroom, but she knew that was probably out of the question. After what felt like hours—but was only 20 minutes—she hadn't found anything of note. But then she noticed another room.

"Oh…" was all Rosie said and then she was silent for a few beats.

"What, what is it? Are you OK?" Jackie asked, a little frantic.

"There's another room. But it has a lock on the door. It's one of those old door knobs with a built-in lock. It needs a key," Rosie said. She gently tugged at the knob just to see if it would give. It didn't.

"OK. I'm googling how to pick an antique doorknob. Hang on," Jackie said. Rosie gulped. Breaking into the house had been terrifying but with the back door unlocked it felt a little less like she was breaking the rules. Picking a lock felt different somehow, which she realized was stupid, she was already in a stranger's house uninvited. But still.

"You need a bobby pin or a paper clip. Do you have either of those?" Jackie asked.

"No. But I'll look around," Rosie said. She headed back toward the kitchen. Almost every house had what she would call a junk drawer. Maybe she'd even find the key. Still with her gloves on, she opened a few drawers until she found one full of miscellaneous things like batteries, pens, a first aid kit, and small tools. She found a screw driver and then it hit her.

"I'm not going to pick the lock. I'm just going to remove the knob from the door," she said into the phone, which was now on speaker phone as she set it nearby and got to work unscrewing anything on the door she could.

"Go Rosie go!" Jackie cheered. And within a few minutes the entire knob and lock was off the door.

"I got it. Wow. OK, I'm going in," Rosie said as she pushed open the door.

Joan rose as she saw Pam enter the coffee shop. She looked different from the few photos Joan had seen of her online; a little older and maybe a little more tired. Joan pushed this from her mind. Pam walked across the small shop to greet her. She reached her arm out to shake her hand, and Joan shook it.

"Sorry I'm a little late. Have you been here long?" Pam asked, eyeing Joan's empty cup.

Thinking quickly Joan responded, "Yes. I misjudged the drive. So I got here a little early. This shop is so quaint. Honestly it almost feels like it could be a part of Brooklyn."

"Yes, you recently moved from there, right? To LA?" Pam asked. Joan felt a jolt of panic at Pam knowing this pretty easy-to-learn detail about her. It made her feel like she wasn't the one doing the interviewing. But of course, Pam had no idea why Joan was really here. She had no idea her friends were probably inside her house right now. Joan calmed down. Her job was to get this woman to talk for at least an hour or more, which she could do.

"Yes, that's right. Can I buy you a drink? I think I'll get another," Joan said as she stood.

"Thank you. I'd love a mocha," Pam said as she sat down.

The women got their drinks, and Joan had ordered a couple slices of pie too. Pam told her how she knew the gal who owned the pie shop in town, and these were made by her. They were probably delicious, but everything tasted like nothing to Joan. The coffee and pie just registered as textures only in her mouth. She hadn't been this nervous in an interview since she'd visited a prison for a story years ago. She hoped it didn't show. She asked a few questions about the town, how long Pam had lived there, what her life was like. She got a few interesting details. Pam worked at a plant nursery. She was divorced and was single. She seemed very, well, normal. But what had Joan expected?

"Do you mind if I take notes?" she asked as she pulled out her little notebook. She flipped to the interview questions she, Jackie, and Rosie had come up with.

"Of course, feel free," Pam said as she took another bite of the pie. Joan started in on some of the more basic questions. When did you first start selling online? When did it first start to work well for you, was there a tipping point or anything that made sales go up? Do you work with influencers, do you consider yourself an influencer? Pam's answers were thoughtful and interesting. It was actually turning out to be a pretty good interview even though it was fake.

"One of the best things I ever did was sending influencers gifts as a way to get promotion. It's a super common practice, and not everyone participates, which is normal," Pam explained. Joan's ears perked up.

"Tell me more. Is it always people you follow you send the gifts to? And how does that translate into promotion?"

"I follow a lot of people online, trying to network I guess. And sometimes I send a message and offer to send them something. It's totally free, just a gift. If they say yes, oftentimes they post about it and when they do then all their followers see my work. If the influencer tags me or mentions my shop name then I almost always see more sales. Sometimes a lot of sales," Pam explained.

"Do you ever send gifts and they don't post about it?"

"Sure. But that's part of it. It's normal. Maybe they forgot. Maybe they didn't like the gift I sent, like it wasn't their color or something. Maybe they never ended up using it. I don't know. Could be a lot of things. It's really not a big deal," Pam said. Although Joan thought she heard something beneath the words, she decided not to push. She wanted Pam to feel good, to talk as long as possible.

"How do you know who to send a gift to? Do you go by their follower count, or if you think their audience will like your style of products? Sounds like a lot of research," Joan said.

"I don't really have a formula. But I guess it's partly about engagement, so like how much people comment on their posts or interact with them. Some influencers have massive followings but not a lot of engagement, which usually means they don't translate to sales as people are watching them passively rather than being involved with them," Pam explained.

"Interesting. I wonder, if an influencer gets too big, and what I mean is a large number of followers, if people feel like they won't get access to them and maybe then don't comment or engage as much?" Joan could feel herself actually getting very curious.

"Probably. Again, I'm really no expert. Just someone who's online probably more than is mentally healthy," Pam said with a laugh. Joan smiled in response. Pam was probably right, she thought.

Rosie was shocked by what she found in the locked bedroom. She felt sick. The room was decorated like a baby's nursery, complete with a crib and mobile hung above. But it was clear by the room and the rest of the house that no baby lived here. She also saw the room was only half a nursery, the other half was a sewing room. It was messy. She started to look through it as she heard Jackie on the other end of the phone.

"What do you see, keep narrating. I get scared when you go quiet."

"Sorry. It's a baby nursery and maybe her work space? I'm looking through the desk right now. There's a sewing machine and lots of different piles of fabric and thread and things like that. There's also this kind of science looking kit, I don't know how to describe it. I'm just going to start taking photos. I think there's something here," Rosie said. She started gently moving things around, opening desk drawers. She figured with the lock removed from the door the jig was kind of up on not touching anything. She snapped photos of everything, not even totally registering what she was seeing. She also felt the pressure of time. She knew it had been at least 40 minutes and she'd need to start wrapping up soon just in case Pam returned.

"Holy shit!" Rosie breathed.

"What? What's happening?" Jackie nearly yelled into the speaker.

"It's bath bomb making supplies. It's the molds and everything," Rosie said as she snapped more photos. She pulled the bottom drawer open and took out a worn notebook. It was full of addresses and dates. She had a scary guess what they meant. She snapped a photo and put the notebook back, explaining everything to Jackie as she did.

"Does she have a computer somewhere?" Jackie asked.

"Yes, it was in her bedroom. I'm not a hacker though. I doubt I can guess her password," Rosie said as she left the nursery room and retrieved the laptop. Sure enough, the screen was locked.

"I bet that's what we need, what she does online. Who she talks to, her emails, that kind of stuff," Jackie said.

"Probably. But that's way beyond my skill level. I honestly can't believe I got the door knob off," Rosie said, shutting the laptop and leaving it as she had found it. She started to head back toward the nursery room when she saw it.

"Jackie, there's a package by the front door. It's packaged up like she's going to mail it soon." Rosie said as she approached it. It looked exactly like the package she had just received. She snapped a photo of it showing the surrounding room.

"Rosie. Get out. She's walking back," Jackie said. Immediately a text popped up on her phone from Joan, saying Pam had left and was heading back. Rosie froze in panic.

"What do I do? I can't let her mail this," Rosie said into the phone.

"Focus. Put everything back as it was and get out now. Go out the back door. I'll intercept her somehow," Jackie said. Rosie began to protest but could hear the car door opening. Jackie had left her on speaker but was clearly already heading toward Pam. Rosie could hear her, although a little muffled and far away sounding.

"Excuse me, do you know where a coffee shop that's around here is? I'm supposed to meet someone there, but I think I parked a little far and now I am not sure where it is," Jackie said. Rosie couldn't hear Pam's response, but she could tell she was talking to her, giving her directions. She moved as quickly as her too-pregnant body would allow. She put the room back as best she could and shut the door, there was no time to put the knob back on, she tried to make it look like it had fallen off. Before she ran to the back door she grabbed the package. This was technically stealing now, but she couldn't let someone else get this package. She tucked it under her arm as she pulled the back door shut as quickly and quietly as she could manage. She could hear Jackie asking Pam to show her which way the coffee shop was, she knew they were probably on the corner. She ducked out of the backyard and onto the street, walking in the opposite direction. She couldn't let Pam see her, since she would know who she was. She hung up the phone just before a dog barked at her. She nearly jumped and dropped the package but didn't. She turned the corner and was out of sight.

"No problem, happy to help," Pam said to the stranger as they headed toward the coffee shop and Pam turned to go back into her home. She was still a little high from the interview. She felt like she'd really hit it off with Joan. But she'd started to feel really sick again and had wanted to get home. She rushed inside and immediately went to the bathroom where she threw up. Maybe the pie hadn't agreed with her. As she rinsed out her mouth she saw the little plastic bag still sitting where she'd shoved it earlier. The thought nagged at her again. Time to put this dumb worry to rest, she thought. She pulled out the box and read the directions. She peed on the stick and then set it on the counter to wait for her results. She scrolled her phone while she waited. She wondered if Rosie had gotten her second package; she'd never sent a second one before. It was too careless of a mistake she wouldn't make again but so far there was nothing of note on Rosie's account. So probably another thing she shouldn't worry about. Restless, she got up and walked toward her kitchen to get a drink. Out of the corner of her eye she saw something. The door knob to her studio was on the ground. Pam felt her pulse quicken, it was weird. Could it have fallen off? No, the screws were sitting neatly beside it. And then her gaze turned toward the front door. The package she had just wrapped up this morning, hours ago, was gone.

"Fuck," she heard herself say aloud. She felt her phone buzz, the timer going off. It made her jump. In a trance she walked back to the bathroom and picked up the test. She was pregnant.

EPILOGUE

Ela
@justanotherela

| **58** POSTS | **2.3M** FOLLOWERS | **832** FOLLOWING |

Pamela walked into the courtroom. As soon as she took a step inside the sterile room went completely quiet, so quiet she could hear her soft sole shoes step across the floor. One step squeaked, and she winced because it seemed so loud. She self-consciously tugged at her dress, it was tight across her already full belly. She knew this was intentional, her lawyer thought they shouldn't hide the pregnancy. Pam didn't know if she agreed with this strategy, but there was no hiding it anyway. She still didn't know if she wanted to be pregnant, but the accused had even less reproductive rights than the general population, it turned out.

Even though she was incredibly isolated in jail she knew what they were saying about her. The world hated her. She was the ultimate villain. She was not surprised by this from those who seemed to believe in life at conception. Fox News really hated her, she was worse than Hitler according to them. And then she'd been really surprised to find she had a small group of, well, fans. Some of the more staunch antinatalists seem to hold her up as some kind of hero; a crusader for a cause that was finally getting the attention it deserved. Although they were usually quick to say they didn't agree with her actions, just her ideology. But what was ideology without action behind it, she wondered.

She felt a sharp nudge to her ribs as her lawyer elbowed her. She realized she'd zoned out. The judge had been talking to her. She was surprised to find she was standing, as was her lawyer and her assistant.

"How do you plead?" he repeated.

"Not guilty," she said. The room started to buzz. There were gasps, then murmurs that quickly turned to yells. The judge slammed her gavel multiple times calling out, "Order. I will close this trial down if those present can't control themselves." Pam wished she would. She didn't dare look around her, but she knew there were women there who she had mailed bath bombs to, and their families. There were also cameras. She felt trapped in her body, and in this room. Like she was a weird science experiment under a microscope lens. Some kind of new virus that doctors looked at with alarm and awe. She had hoped for a plea deal, but there had been no offer. Her lawyer had been surprised. Pam could tell she was worried and not very experienced. Just her luck. Melissa Drexler had pled guilty to manslaughter after throwing her baby away in a trash can and gotten 15 years, in the end only serving three. But Pam suspected Drexler didn't get quite the media treatment she was getting. She squirmed in her chair, she wished she could go pee.

Joan sat in the window of a coffee shop across the street from the courthouse. The scene out there was like a circus, absolute chaos. She knew she shouldn't linger. She should sip her coffee and leave so other customers who wanted to watch the courthouse could have her seat. She could hardly bring herself to join the crowd, although she was as much a part of the media as anyone. It had been her podcast that had broken the story after all. She also had been the only one to interview Pam so far.

As she walked past the edges of the crowd, vying for a quiet space to watch and gather her thoughts, she heard some of the reporters recording their intros and B-reel. They were calling Pamela the hand-made murderess. Some called her the bath bomb baby killer. Often, they got her actual name wrong. And although Pam was no longer on social media, as she wasn't allowed to use it while she was in jail, Joan had seen her profile now had over two million followers. It was interesting to think people would follow someone out of hate or disgust. And while Joan felt confident Pam had indeed committed the acts she was on trial for, she couldn't help but feel there was no way she would get a fair trial. Her case was already way too famous for her to actually be innocent until proven guilty. And Joan knew this was, at least in part, because of her. She felt a strange mixture of guilt tied to her reporting, even if she knew she and Rosie and Jackie (not to mention Abby, Carmen, Leena, and all the others) had stopped Pam from hurting anyone else. It was all so messy and complicated, in a way Joan hadn't encountered before. It felt heavy, like a weighted blanket you couldn't take off. She let out a long sigh, before she pressed the record button.

ACKNOWLEDGEMENTS

This book would not exist without the support of so many wonderful people.

My first readers: Elsie Larson, Trey George, and Michelle Houghton. Honestly, I probably wouldn't have published this without your encouragement and it certainly would not have been as good as it is without your notes. Elsie, you have always been my biggest and probably most enthusiastic cheerleader. I got very lucky to have a sister like you. I hope we create lots more together and separately so I can cheerlead for you. Trey, you helped shape this book to be so much better! I love how you can spot a reveal a mile away, it makes me work that much harder to try and surprise you. And when I fail, you help me make it better. Thank you. I love you. Michelle, there are not many friends with plates as full as yours who would make the time to read an early draft and offer such thoughtful (and kind! and specific!) notes to a friend. It means a lot, truly.

Lindsay Edgecombe, your encouragement and willingness to give me notes on my pitch were helpful even though I went a different direction. I will always value your time and opinion and you have always given it to me so generously. Lucky, lucky me.

Mara Dockery, you made the cover design for this book SO good! You always make my projects so much better than I imagined. Thank you.

Kelsey Baldwin, not only did you thoughtfully and carefully layout this book, your help with the self-publishing process was so valuable to me. You don't know how grateful I am to have smart, talented friends to work with.

Sarah Jenkins, you know how terrible at spelling and grammar I am since you proofed this book. Please take this knowledge to your grave. I would hate for my past English teachers to know how much they failed me. Thank you in advance.

To my book club, a.k.a. Girls Group, thank you for your love and encouragement. I would be so alone without you. I love you.

Mom and Dad, thank you for a childhood filled with adventure and creativity. I have always known I was unconditionally loved by you and it's the best safety net in the world. You taught me creative work is about the process, not the end result, and to have fun. I had a lot of fun writing this weird, creepy book. I love you both.

ABOUT THE AUTHOR

PHOTO BY JANAE HARDY

Emma Chapman is a blogger and podcast host based in
Springfield, Missouri where she lives with her husband,
toddler son, dog Steve, and ghost dog Lovers.

Printed in Great Britain
by Amazon

31946197R00128